MURDER AT LAKE ONTARIO

Detective William Gibson returns in this gripping murder mystery

KATHY GARTHWAITE

THE
BOOK
FOLKS

Paperback edition published by

The Book Folks

London, 2019

© Kathy Garthwaite

This book is a work of fiction. Names, characters, businesses, organizations, places and events are either the product of the author's imagination or are used fictitiously. Any resemblance to actual persons, living or dead, events or locales is entirely coincidental. The spelling is British English.

All rights reserved. No part of this publication may be reproduced, stored in retrieval system, copied in any form or by any means, electronic, mechanical, photocopying, recording or otherwise transmitted without written permission from the publisher.

ISBN 978-1-0973-0596-4

www.thebookfolks.com

To my Dad.
Who inspired me to love to read.

Prologue

Summer in the eastern regions of Canada was all about sunshine and water.

Lawsons Lane had plenty of both for the children that lived there. A dead-end street with steps leading down to a pristine sandy shore. Cars that slowed for the bicycles swinging side to side on the dusty track. Large grassy meadows to run through and hide. Squeals of laughter and joy from the early light of morning through the sweltering heat of the day, ending in exhaustion as the sun dipped behind the escarpment to the west.

It was considered to be a safe place to raise a family until a bike was found on the landing above the beach, and a young girl vanished into thin air.

A lone figure placed the shovel on the wall, where an outline in black marked its proper spot, and joined the frantic throng in search of the lost child.

Bees droned overhead, and birds darted across azure skies.

The first death on Lawsons Lane. They said it was a drowning.

Chapter 1

Inspector William Gibson was eager to get on the plane to Ontario. On this special assignment to his old stomping grounds, he would furnish the glue to integrate the Niagara Peninsula Major Crimes Task Force with Inspector Rene Eckhart at the helm.

But Gibson had an ulterior motive for wanting this trip so badly. His good buddy had let slip something that had stunned him. He wavered on the truth of what he had been told, but it made sense now that he thought about it. And his buddy had grown up in the same small town, had been a banker there all his life and knew a lot of people. The man would know.

Gibson was glad that this was a solitary jaunt. Not only because he wanted to find answers, but he needed some time for himself. The last year had been a stormy one. The cases, arduous. His wife's panic attacks, draining. Life at home with Katherine had become a plodding routine. A fragment of love persisted, but an aching hollowness thrust away the light. A sad smile flickered and snuffed out. He settled into the generous-sized seat, an extra pillow behind his head and a good deal of room to spread his long limbs, and nudged aside his sense of guilt. With half-closed eyelids, he tuned in to the strum of the jet stream, morphing into a percussion of breakers on a craggy seashore. Pictures of kayaks zigzagging through never-ending nooks and crannies along the coastal inlets flooded his imagination. He gradually ebbed away, wrapped in the delicious comfort of sleep.

The sticky, squelchy sound of rubber hitting tarmac stirred Gibson from his dreams. He peered out the tiny window. Waves of heat steaming off the runway distorted the view. It must be boiling out there. He grabbed his knapsack from the overhead locker and headed down the aisle. After a quick jog along a lengthy corridor, circumventing the baggage carousel, he finally reached the arrival area and out the door.

The heat hit his cheek like a slap, but not as hard as what he saw before him—a Ford Expedition with a NPMCTF emblem painted on the door, its left front tire jumped up on the curb and a drop-dead gorgeous woman leaning against the hood. Her willowy body had sun-kissed skin of bronze. Rosy swipes of colour splashed across her high cheekbones. Amber gold hair tumbled in waves to her shoulders. Dark pools of blue, the hue of an ocean pulsating, stared out from under flickering lashes. A sensuous hint of mischief sculpted her pale pink lips. Gibson caught his breath. She smiled.

It was his ride, Inspector Eckhart. Rene, not a man—definitely not a man. He held out a palm, and she took the invitation. A zip of electricity traveled up his arm. He put his trembling hand into his jeans pocket and jerked his eyes from the deep pools, choosing not to drown. Not yet anyway.

"Pleased to meet you at last," she said.

"Me, too."

His feet felt leaden.

"This is my ride. Let's go." She tapped the hood and flashed him an encouraging smile.

"Great." Gibson threw his bag in the rear and hopped in.

First in line. First out. Eckhart hit the turnpike before the hordes had picked out their luggage. She drove down the eight-lane highway at a clip. Gibson eased back into his seat and listened to her chitchat. Her voice was melodious, a bubbling mountain creek. The truck slipped out of the hustle of the city. Their destination was an hour in time—a century away from the insidious gloom of Toronto. Soon they neared St. Catharines. She cruised the backroads to the Task Force. The scenery rolled by—the flatness of the region sporadically broken by groves of woods. Out west, his beloved conifers shot up higher than skyscrapers, the coastal rains sustaining their growth. Here the trees were limited, restrained by severe winter storms and summer drought.

On the outskirts of town, the landscape shifted into commercial zone blandness, which really meant plain buildings and pavement. She pulled into the station parking lot. The red brick structure was a squat one-storey affair extended over an entire block. Windows mirrored the dazzling sunlight. The temperature had rocketed past the mid 30s as the day drew on. A mist rising above each vehicle hood produced a delusion of fluctuating images. A large Ford F150 with a Royal Canadian Mounted Police logo sat crosswise at the entrance.

"That'll be Rodney," Eckhart said.

"The boss."

"Yup. The superintendent."

A swipe of the electronic key and the entry clicked open. It was nice to step out of the heat into a refreshing lobby. The front desk was empty. Muffled voices slipped through a cracked door at the rear.

"We haven't got a receptionist. But soon enough." She gave a shrug. "There's still lots to do, but we're getting there. You should meet the officers first. Rodney is probably with them."

She traipsed across the immense space, shoes clicking on the tile floor, and peered in a doorway.

"Hi, guys. Inspector Gibson is here."

Three men popped out of the room. Superintendent Rodney Snowden was a burly fellow with a rugged complexion. The hand he held out to Gibson felt like worn leather. A man of the street. Same as him.

"Welcome. Moreover, thanks for coming. Really." The baritone voice was reassuring. A youthful confidence sparked his hickory brown eyes. His laughter rolled.

"We'll spin this into an ass-kicking crime unit," William said and gestured, collecting in the full place with a sweep of his hand. He wavered for a moment. "East of the Rockies." And he meant it.

"Yes, sir." DC Peter Jones let out a throaty laugh, his smile revealing a top row of perfect teeth.

DC Ron Cooper nodded, and the two men bumped fists.

"So is your wife at the motel resting or has she gone shopping?" Rodney asked. A wide grin forming thick lines from his mouth got swallowed up by the craters in his cheeks.

"Actually, I came here on my own."

"So, you're an old married man."

"No. We've only been married for two years."

"Second marriage would be my guess?"

"Yeah." Gibson shuffled his feet, wishing the cross-examination would be over soon. His first wife was something he didn't want to think about. It had ended in disaster—from the marriage bed to the couch to the divorce court.

"Any kids?" Rodney's smile warmed another degree.

"We're trying." Gibson glanced at the screen when his cell chirped, but he swiped the 'ignore' button and put the phone back in his pocket.

"No kids from your first marriage?"

Gibson shook his head.

"Sorry. I can't help myself. My wife tells me that I grill everybody I meet. That's why I don't have any friends." He laughed. "I hope you can get along with my inspector. Have fun with it." He headed for the door, letting in a whoosh of hot air.

Eckhart glanced sideways at Gibson and licked her lips.

"You bet. I'll do my best to be of service," Gibson said to the retreating superintendent.

"Shall we do a tour?" Eckhart asked.

Gibson lowered his head and exhaled loudly.

"You're hungry?"

"Yeah."

"Let's go."

Chapter 2

The muggy heat persisted even as the light faded, turning blue skies to black. Rivers of fiery sparks streamed across the canvas of midnight. Each explosive crack drew a new pattern into the sky, releasing fingers of vivid colour. Brilliant trails swept to the horizon and disappeared. The drama concluded with a progression of snaps and booms. They burst into silvers and reds, celebrating Canada Day. The revelers cheered as the flashes whipped across the heavens for the final hurrah, leaving smoke to linger.

"How about a stroll on the beach?" David Hunter asked as he seized his wife's hand.

"Sure," Jackie answered.

They walked in silence toward the lake, the mere hint of a breeze—almost as warm as the night air—giving no relief as it brushed their sunburned faces. The moonlight paled against the wealth of stars above, and the lone light in the distance was a beacon for the shore below. An occasional tweet from the shrubbery along the shoulder of the lonely lane, and the far-off timbre of waves lapping the shoreline were muted sounds in the background.

A cry chopped the stillness into tiny pieces of fear. David and Jackie came to a standstill on the landing.

"Look out!" Gregory Cunningham screamed as he staggered up the rickety stairs. He howled as his foot caught on a jagged board, and his knee struck a stray nail on the top step. He scrambled up quickly, knocking Jackie against the post. David stood in his way, but Gregory jammed him with an elbow to move.

"Elsie's dead."

Jackie drew in her breath.

"What are you talking about? Slow down." David snatched the young man's wrist. The stickiness was warm.

"At the bottom. I don't know." Gregory squirmed in David's grip. "Let me go." He wrenched himself free and sprinted off into the dimness, a faint shape in the dusk as he slipped away.

"Gregory!" Jackie shouted. "Where are you going?" With clenched teeth, she held back a scream latched deep in her throat. Her pulse throbbed with a fuzzy pitch in her ears. She hung onto the railing, her brain spinning and the lightness in her limbs threatening to let her down.

"Are you okay?" David asked.

She nodded.

"Stay here!" The tremor in David's voice bordered on panic. He fought it and plunged into the dark abyss where some kind of terror waited.

Jackie remained paralyzed. David's hurried footfalls vibrated on the waterlogged wood and echoed against the dunes. Then nothing but a deathly silence, punctuated by her stifled sobs, filled the empty night; her body quivering like a lost kitten in the rain. A scraping sound from the nearby bushes was all it took to send her flying down the stairs just moments after David had taken the leap into the unknown. She careened off the bottom step and landed on the soft sand next to him. At their feet lay their friend, Elsie Webber. Her long, loose skirt billowed out, revealing flabby thighs and stiff sandals. Her curly ruby locks that had tumbled around her satin complexion that same afternoon, were now matted in a brew of blood and grime.

David dropped to his knees and hovered his palm over the figure. He gulped and stretched his fingers to her neck.

"Shit. There's no pulse." He yanked his hand aside as if he had touched a pot of boiling water.

"Did she fall?" Jackie's thoughts swirled like a black mist at the edges of her mind.

"How would I know?" His voice hit a shrill note that skipped across the lake.

Jackie had a sudden urge to flee. She flinched at a sound in the undergrowth, but it was only restless birds fighting for the best roost.

David fell back on his calves and pulled out his cell. His trembling fingers loosened, sending the phone into the sand. He scooped it up and dialed 911.

"There's been an accident on Lawsons Lane. On the beach."

He hung up and stared at his wife.

"Do we have to stay here?" she asked.

"No. We'll wait on the landing."

Jackie took a last look at her friend as she trudged up the wooden slats. She wiped away the surge of tears and put on a brave face, waiting for the ambulance, hoping. The sirens ripped through the night, fading in and out at each bend of the road. A dozen headlights swarmed at the top of the street, bearing down on them, and pressing into the darkness. Invariably, the noise and lights attracted a mob. David blocked the entrance, holding them into submission with a low-pitched hiss.

"Back off."

They pushed against David. More partygoers from the fireworks display arrived like slow drops of water from a leaky faucet, seeking a morbid distraction. The air was charged with a palpable murmur as rumours whizzed in a rage of wildfires, skipping from mouth to ear to the husband—Todd, who pounded down the narrow lane, barging through a flash of selfies, his blood ablaze. He hurtled through obstacles in his path, crashing into David's feeble barrier and barreling past him. The steps rattled with the force of his hammering feet as he plunged to his destiny. David pitched into the void right behind him. A penetrating shriek resonated all around.

An unmarked vehicle pulled up to the landing and DC Cooper jumped out. He ran down the steps and returned within a few minutes as emergency vehicles crammed into the narrow space. Another sound made Jackie turn to face Savannah Jacobs, Elsie's sister, who had staggered to a halt, panting from a hard run to reach the waterfront. Jackie reached out too late and watched as her friend fell into a heap in the dirt. The last thing she heard was the officer shouting into his cell phone.

"Where the hell is Inspector Eckhart? We have a homicide."

* * *

The light faded quickly into a dusk that still held onto the heat as Eckhart drove down the service roads to Port Dalhousie. She parked on a side street, and she and Gibson headed down an alleyway covered with cobblestone. An oversized banana plant stood at the entrance of a seafood restaurant tucked in at the rear. The double oak doors were carved with whales. Large brass handles resembling mermaids carried the theme. In the foyer, several ficus plants in giant pots shielded the tables from the reservation desk. A girl dressed in white slacks and a bright tunic stamped with seahorses greeted them with a preppy smile. They followed her up a short flight of steps to a smaller room. Voices babbled happily and laughter filled the room. They relaxed on wooden chairs, knees touching under the wobbly table. A red and white checkerboard tablecloth placed diagonally hung almost to the floor. One lit candle in a glass jar and a single rose in a slim vase set the atmosphere.

"What do you think?" Eckhart asked.

"Charming."

"Best fish tacos ever." She glimpsed up at him and smiled. "This side of the Rockies."

"Is that right?" He felt the warmth of her body across the table.

The waiter came and went unnoticed, leaving behind a platter of food. Eckhart munched on a crisp taco; sauce dripped from the side of her mouth. She dabbed her lips with a napkin.

"It's good," Gibson said as he bit into a nacho. His cell chirped again. He looked at the screen and shut it off.

"Nothing important?" She put her phone on vibrate and stuck it in her purse. "Me neither."

Gibson smiled his quirky smile and took another bite.

"What now? Can I entice you to my place for a nightcap?" Eckhart asked after the table was cleared and they were ready to leave.

A burst of light lit up the skies over the lake. They both looked up as the colours trickled through the blackness.

"I forgot it was a holiday," Gibson said.

"Well?" Her blue eyes sparkled.

"It's been a long day for me. I should get some sleep." He hesitated about taking the first dip in the pool.

"Okay." She pushed her lips into an exaggerated pout.

Gibson waited on the sidewalk for his cab and watched wistfully as Eckhart drove off. Within a half an hour, he was settled in his room on Lakeshore Road, resting into the comfy mattress, his pillow fluffed up and a big lump of guilt in his gut. He looked at his phone and saw that he had missed three calls and a couple of texts from Katherine. He thought about what he had done in the past and wondered if he was destined to repeat his behaviour. And yes, here he was in the Western Motel thinking about Eckhart, not his wife. Perspiration gathered on his brow when a picture of Katherine entered his mind. What am I doing? He brushed at his forehead to remove the moisture. Or possibly his shame? He twirled his wedding band around his finger several times before he took it off and placed it on the night table. The roar of cars on the busy street bombarded the motel sliding door, slipping through the small fissures, adding to the white noise from the air conditioning and lulled him to sleep.

Chapter 3

A glimmer of light snuck through a crack in the drawn shades. Eckhart heard a buzzing sound and saw her purse jumping madly on the night table. She reached over a glass to snag the cell when her hand knocked the remote to the floor with a crash, sailing it across the room. The volume button caught the side of an armchair, and an automobile chase down the streets of San Francisco blasted from the television.

"Ah, shit. Go figure." She slid off the bed and jammed at the toggle, prepared to hurl it out the window. Silence, at last.

"Eckhart."

"There's been a murder," Cooper said.

"Where?"

"Lawsons Lane."

"I'm on my way." She hung up and dialed the inspector.

"Gibson."

"It's me. There's been a murder."

"What?"

"I'll come get you."

"Okay. I'm at Just Roasted Cafe. Do you know the coffee shop on Lakeshore?"

"Yeah. Won't be long."

Eckhart stepped outside to a white light that washed the sky of its blue. Dawn had abandoned its coolness to the sustained warmth from the day before. A blistering sun beat down without mercy. Birds holed up in still foliage sounded random trills in revolt. She fired up the truck praying the vents would bring relief from the stifling air. Her sunglasses dropped to the floor as she wrestled with the overhead compartment. She picked them up. One of the lenses had cracked.

"Shit. It's going to be one of those days." She tossed the sunglasses into the centre console.

Her skin glistened, and the nape of her neck was already damp. She mopped at a bead of perspiration on her forehead and headed out of Port Dalhousie. The waterfront neighborhood was undergoing rapid gentrification. Fifties houses fought in a battle with new multi-storey condominiums. Vivid greens, pinks and yellows splashed storefront buildings. Developers were the big winners.

Eckhart zipped across the bridge that spanned Martindale Pond. The powder-blue water paralleled the colourless sky. Since 1903 the Royal Canadian Henley Regatta had called this pond their home. She had enjoyed viewing the race, and the rowers' muscular calves and sculpted arms. She pulled around the intersection and hopped the curb. Gibson darted out of the café and jumped into the passenger seat.

"What a nightmare." She leaned in and whiffed a scent of musk aftershave.

"What happened?"

"I don't know yet. I just got the call."

"When did it happen?"

"It was last night. I didn't have my phone on." Her sultry gaze flitted to Gibson and down to his hand, a white mark where his ring should have been.

He looked away from the subtlety of her remark, a blush rising behind his collar.

Bright sunlight reflected off the road, causing a feathery haze that wavered in her eyes. Eckhart drove down Lakeshore Road through the suburbs to a vertical-lift bridge over the Welland Canal. The man-made forty-three-kilometre shipping lane traversed the Niagara Peninsula from Port Weller to Port Colborne connecting Lakes Ontario and Erie. It was a bypass of the Falls providing ships passage through the Great Lakes system by its eight locks. Gibson gazed down the canal as they passed over, the tires singing on the crisscross steel grate. A black bow rose high in the air, giving the sense it would spill onto the roadway. He cringed at its colossal size. In the other direction, a ribbon of water glimmered in the sunlight along the flat landscape.

Eckhart proceeded on past the East-West Road, flying by a few vineyards and fire lanes. The Expedition bounded over the uneven roads without any problems. As she rounded the next corner, the Jacobs Landing sign cropped up in the distance. The yellow and red board was pinned to a steel pole adjacent to the street. In the bottom right-hand corner, it read *Since 1945*. She turned left onto Lawsons Lane and sped toward the waterfront.

DC Jones leaned on a post wiping the glow from his brow with his shirttail, although fresh beads developed immediately. He stabbed out his tongue and panted. Eckhart spun to a stop metres away, corkscrewing dust into his face.

"Sorry," she shouted and lifted her hands in surrender. A smirk pulled up a lip at the corner.

Jones shrugged it off, brushing at his pants. Gibson stepped out into the absolute heat. A light burst of refreshing air surged past him off the lake below, not salty like his beloved Pacific Ocean, but cooling.

"That's better," he said.

"Yes, sir. It's a bit of relief," Jones agreed.

Eckhart dipped her chin and accompanied Gibson down the shaky stairs. The detectives leaped off the final step. Yellow tape surrounded an indentation in the dark-stained sand. Cooper hunkered in the shade of shrubbery against the bank. He scrambled over to stand with the bosses. The scorched sand shimmered silvery diamonds. Gibson placed his hand on his forehead to ward off the glare and gazed across the wind-ruffled water, keeping his face up to detect the puffs of air. It was a wrestle between the sunlight and the breeze. He longed for the balmy temperate weather of the coast. Here it was thirty-three degrees and climbing. He wiped his brow again.

"So, what happened here?" Eckhart asked.

"There was a firework display on the property at the top of the stairs. On the left. A couple came down after the party for a stroll on the beach." He looked at his notes. "The guy phoned it in, but he wasn't the person who found the body. That was a Gregory Cunningham."

"Who is the victim?"

"Elsie Webber. She runs the store at Jacobs Landing along with her husband, Todd." He pressed his lips together.

"Anything else you can tell us?"

He shook his head.

"Okay. We'll head over to the morgue." She could sense that Cooper wanted to ask her something by the way he was fidgeting. She wasn't going to tell him why her cellphone wasn't on.

"Should Jones and I head back to the station? There's nothing left for us to do here. All the evidence was taken to the lab."

"Has Todd been notified?"

"Yeah. He was here last night."

"Here. Like at the party?"

"No. On the beach."

She nodded and turned to walk away.

The cooling breeze had died. The buzz of flies around the blood in the sand grew louder.

Chapter 4

A lazy breeze fluttered the curtains, and a spicy fragrance of the honeysuckle on the trellis drifted in through the open window. David rubbed his tired eyes and raked his fingers through his unruly hair. The sun had barely risen. He sat on the edge of the couch, elbows on his thighs, hands held in prayer at his mouth. The flaming sphere breached the horizon and shattered the blues of the night. Streaks of sunlight zinged through the glass. The brilliance clawed at his face, his eyelids flickered. Not a cloud in the sky to check it. He pulled himself up and trotted across the scarred wooden floor, arms crisscrossed over his barrel of a trunk.

An indistinct movement and the hint of a squeak made Jackie stir from an edgy rest. She opened her eyes lethargically inhaling the dread of the night before. A flat but regular breathing emanated from the bed where Savannah took cover under a scattering of sheets. Her cheeks puffed with each rise and fall of her rib cage. Jackie let the blanket she had clung onto for security all night slide to the ground. One final look and she tiptoed out of the bedroom.

"Hi." She stretched her arms to shake off the tiredness that lingered.

"Should we go?" David looked down at his dusty toes. He uncrossed his arms and reached for her arm, stopping midway. "Are you all right?"

What a dumb question. None of them were okay. They gathered their meagre belongings and stepped out the door, the heat forcing into them like an unwanted visitor.

"Uber?"

"Let's hope so. We should have driven ourselves."

David dialed from his phone app. He crossed his fingers. Thank goodness someone answered. They waited fifteen minutes in the shade of the store veranda, one that may never open again. A white Acura SUV glided into the parking lot. A youthful fellow rolled down the window.

"Hi, hop in."

"Thanks."

"Where to?"

"Denver Court. Do you know it?"

"Yup." The driver glanced in the rear. "I heard about the murder on the radio this morning. An acquaintance of yours?"

"Yeah," Jackie answered, her swollen eyes testament to her grief.

The driver was stunned at her reply and remained quiet. He managed a U-turn in the lane and veered right at the stop sign heading toward town.

Jackie glanced over to David, but he was slumped back into his seat with his eyes closed. She looked out the window. They pushed past Grantham Avenue with a mall on three of its corners and took a left on Niagara Road with its row of plane trees, a memorial to the First World War veterans. They sailed by a neighbourhood of deep-rooted money, estates that had passed down to an insolent generation. Tall stone screens and black iron fences hid lush lawns and massive mansions. A line of trees overhung the road making a tunnel of coolness. The leaves swooshed with a wisp of air. Almost home. They rounded the last intersection to the familiar dwelling. The Uber guy dropped them off unceremoniously and reeled out of the cul-de-sac to his next client. They slogged up the driveway. Jackie's mom stared through the screen, a somber expression on her face. Death lurked around the corner.

"Your father's downstairs." Mrs. Abigail Cunningham locked the hotness outside to torment someone else. She fled to the kitchen where she had started the day.

"Hey." Jackie bolted down the steps. Her dad's thick hair was jet black with a smidgen of gray encroaching at the temples, the only notable change in the last decade. The laugh lines, the affectionate grin and soft face provided evidence of his jovial personality.

"How could this happen? Who would have done such a thing? To Elsie? What did she ever do to anybody? Boy-oh-boy," he said.

"Yeah." She leaned in close. Their foreheads touched. "I'll go help mom."

David eased into an orange recliner. Mr. Jonnie Cunningham slumped on the couch, a beer belly overhanging his sweatpants. A sports channel trumpeted in the background.

"Do you fish?" David asked.

"I would like to. Never got around to it. You know, work, kids..." Regret hid behind the older man's laughing eyes.

But David loved the sport so he chattered about his great times hauling in the big one. Anything to keep focused elsewhere and push the harsh reality aside. He listed off his favourite flies: Woolly bugger, Royal Wulff and Adam's Parachute.

"Really. That's a hell of a thing," Jonnie commented. He coughed, inducing his breathing to become erratic.

"Are you okay?" The episode alarmed David.

"It'll pass. I think I'll go lie down for a while."

Upstairs the ladies were at odds, bordering on an argument. The usual conversation with her mother.

"When are you going back to college?"

"Mom."

"You can't be a teacher's helper for the rest of your life. You're smart. You could be a real teacher."

"Yeah, I know."

The babble went on and on. Jackie stared out the wide window at the evergreen hedge surrounding the backyard. It was beautifully sculpted. Had her dad done that? Surely not.

"You were an honour student, for crying out loud."

"I have to freshen up. I parked in an armchair all night," Jackie said and left the kitchen unable to process anything after what had happened to her friend last night. Was there a killer on the loose? It was a disturbing thought.

David heard Jackie in the washroom and took the chance to sneak away for a few minutes. He slipped out the side door and walked quickly down the street and around the corner. With a glance backwards, he figured the coast was clear. He fumbled in his pocket, yanked out a pack of cigarettes and lit up. It was a bad habit from school that he hadn't quite conquered, and resorted to when he felt stressed like he did now. Should he have told someone what he had seen? Who? Jackie? Todd? The police? Now in the bright daylight and looking back to last night, it made him question himself. He wasn't even sure what he saw. David tossed his smoke on the asphalt pulverizing it out with the toe of his shoe and walked back.

Chapter 5

"The morgue is across town. Should we stop for lunch first?" Eckhart asked. "I think we should." She wavered on whether it was better to eat before or after their little visit.

"Okay," Gibson agreed.

She drove down Lakeshore to Niagara Street and onto the overpass of the Queen Elizabeth Highway. Gibson looked down at the vehicles heading from Toronto to the States. It was a constant stream of bumper to bumper traffic at 120 kph.

When they reached downtown, Eckhart had to do a loop to get to St. Paul Street because it was a one-way street. Stupid planning. The main thoroughfare had the expected array of original and contemporary architectures. A revitalization program had recently attracted the hordes fleeing from mundane shopping malls. She hauled into a spot in front of the Mansion Pub. Built in 1806, it was the oldest licensed establishment in Canada. The interior had antique timber beams, wainscoting and parquet floors. Everything wooden with an old-world charm. They sat at the bar on swivel stools, touching elbows—he felt the energy.

Gibson had a New York cheddar and bacon burger, and Eckhart munched on a Reuben sandwich with a side of fries. They passed the time with restrained chatter preferring not to speculate too far ahead of any facts. He read through the notes Cooper had given them—an updated summary of the incident and everybody's name and contact numbers. When they wound up their lunch and strode outside, the sun was more intense.

They headed to the hospital on Fourth Avenue. The morgue was fittingly tucked into the bowels of the building. Eckhart peeped through the small window in the entry door. The glaring overhead lights washed out the green of the walls, which was probably a good thing. Dr. Barrie Staples wore a long white coat over polyester pants, his dark hair was covered with a net. He bustled around his domain, rearranging utensils and flushing the blood-speckled sink. She shuddered and entered, hoping for a quick in and out, so as to reduce her intake of moribund air. Gibson followed.

"Hi. This is Gibson, the detective from BC," Eckhart said.

"Pleased to meet you."

"Same here. Heard you came out to help set up the Task Force."

"Yeah, here I am." Gibson threw his quirky smile and passed his palm through sweat-saturated hair.

"I guess this isn't quite what you planned." The ME tried to maintain a straight face, but it didn't work. He was an upbeat fellow used to the horror of his trade. He chortled and was greeted with silence.

"Okay. I just finished up here. So, let me explain what I encountered." He opened a massive gate on the far wall and hoisted out a stainless-steel tray with Elsie laid out upon it. A toe tag and a white sheet were all she had left. He tugged on the covering to expose her right arm. The purple and yellow marks were dramatic. He pointed to the edges of the bruise that wrapped around her upper arm.

"Here and here. Someone grabbed her first." He pointed to a circle shape with a thumb mark on one side and finger pads on the other.

The detectives nodded.

The ME drew the blanket to her neck and slanted her head to the side, pushing away a lock of hair.

"The head wound is extensive. It's hard to determine the force that was used, but the cut is deep. She got a considerable crack to the temple. Several, actually. The bones of the skull are fractured in two places."

Eckhart gawked at the gash ingrained with sand.

"The initial impact would have killed her. The second one was..."

"Geesh," Eckhart said.

"Sorry." Barrie pushed Elsie back into the refrigerated container.

After thanking the ME, they slipped out of the room and toddled down the passageway, not much to say. Someone had ticketed Eckhart's truck. She snorted a mirthless laugh and tossed it in the back with a few others that had been abandoned in similar circumstances. Gibson wanted to laugh out loud, but he felt a sadness after seeing Elsie. He didn't think he would ever get used to seeing a person laid out like a slab of meat. It wasn't a physical repulsion. It was something more. A loathing of the killer. Like, how dare you extinguish this life?

Eckhart drove back to the station by a different route, one that Gibson didn't know. She remained quiet for the remainder of the ride. Maybe she was thinking the same thing he was.

She fumbled with her card at the door. The lock clacked loudly as it released. They entered an empty building, an eerie stillness. The first room they passed was in disarray with filing cabinets against one wall, their empty drawers hauled out. Folders were showered on the floor with each stack stamped a specific colour, for a particular type of crime. Murder. Kidnapping. Rape.

"That's Cooper's office." A slight smile unfurled across her face, enhancing the cleft below her nose. No teeth showing, just plump pink lips.

The next office was smaller and orderly. Most folders had found their way into the filing cabinet. A bookshelf lined with self-help paperbacks was tucked behind a small writing table.

"Jones is a better housekeeper." She didn't laugh.

Gibson grunted.

"Everyone must be in the lab," Eckhart said.

They walked down the long corridor to the lab technician's department in a rightfully subdued mood.

* * *

Eckhart opened the solid entry with her electronic key, and they entered a windowless space. A hum of machinery purred in the background. Unpacked boxes covered a substantial chunk of the counters. Flasks, beakers, microscopes and homogenizers were assembled ready for action. The two DCs, Cooper and Jones, stood in a semi-circle with the lab technician.

Francis. (Frenchy) Cross was a petite woman, with a heart-shaped face and a short bob haircut. Between the wisps of her fine hair, Gibson could see a tiny Chinese symbol tattooed behind one ear. She wore a long green lab coat, buttoned tight to her neck and no jewelry except for one ring on her right pinky finger.

"Hi, I'm Frenchy. I'll get right to it. That's why you're here. Right?" She gave the slimmest of grins.

Gibson nodded. He liked her already. All business. She looked smart too.

"We have two pieces of evidence from the beach. Let's start with the murder weapon. There is a partial print. So that's good news." Frenchy crossed to a counter halfway across the room. They followed. Top dog and puppy dogs right behind. She stood in front of a glass container with a rock inside. It was a light shade of crimson flecked with dark speckles. "This is an igneous rock. Mostly composed of granite. It's an extremely tough, almost weatherproof stone. That's ideal for us because obtaining a print from a nonporous rock is simpler. That doesn't mean it won't be difficult though. It will be." She paused. "I won't be able to lift a print until the blood is completely stabilized. It will be a few days. If I do it too soon, I'll lose the clarity of the print at best. Might not get anything useful for you at the worst."

"Better to wait, then," Gibson agreed.

She shot him a glance as if to say, doesn't matter what you think.

"I'm not sure if you know this or not, but I'll go over it for you anyway. We have a software development kit that provides multi-biometric fingerprint identification. The ID program matches prints whether they were taken flat or rolled. It's quite a unique kit and very accurate. The finest available." She drew in a breath. "If we could get the software to work, I'd be happy."

"Sorry about that." A lanky young fellow leaped up from behind a partition. "I'm working on it." He peered at them over wire-rimmed glasses and then retreated.

"I know you're doing your best." She frowned.

"Couldn't we send everything to the RCMP Automated Fingerprint Identification System (AFIS) in Toronto?" Eckhart asked.

"Oh, sure we could. And I will if we don't get this thing fixed."

"I'll get it soon." A voice sounded from the corner.

Frenchy whirled and marched to the far end of the room. They followed her like sheep. When she tugged on a handle, the drawer slid free. She fingered a leather pouch and placed it on the surface. With a tip of the bag, a signet ring spilled onto a velvet pad. Then she took out some photographs from the rear of the storage and gave one to each of the officers.

"The ring was found under the body."

"Interesting," Gibson said.

"The inscription around the stone says, 'Alpha Zee'."

"Is that a local fraternity?" Gibson looked at his partner.

"From Grimsby, I believe."

"Do you know who the members are?"

"Not really, but we'll find out," Eckhart promised.

"I couldn't get any prints off it. Even though the ring has been recently buffed, there are too many nicks and scratches. There aren't any initials either. The lettering you can see here says 10K, as in gold."

"Rats. What else do we have?"

"That's it."

"Shit. That's not much help." Eckhart twisted her mouth.

"An RCMP officer…" Cooper stepped forward, drew his journal from his pocket and flipped the pages. He glanced up and proceeded, "A Constable Dufferin gave me a buzz this morning. He was the first officer on the scene. He said a David Hunter was the fellow who called it in."

Gibson's eyebrows shot up. That rang a bell. "Have you got a number?"

"Yeah. They're from BC and staying at the wife's parents' place." Cooper rapped off the information and then stared at his notebook. "Oh, this is a landline. Must be the parents' contact."

"Is his spouse called Jackie?" Gibson asked.

"How did you know?" Cooper produced a sharp snort.

"David's boss was murdered last fall at his workplace."

"Whoa!"

"I'm sure it's just a fluke." Although the detective in him didn't like coincidences. He spun to Eckhart. "Nothing more for us here. Time to hit the pavement."

"Back to work, Jonsey," Cooper said.

"Boring." His buddy jabbed him in the ribs.

They dragged their feet back to the chaotic rubble in Cooper's office.

"See you guys later," Eckhart said as she pulled on the front door. She shielded her eyes from the glare wishing she had sunglasses and jumped into the driver's seat. They sat in the Expedition with the air conditioning on full blast, going over their course of action.

"We'll talk to David and Jackie first. We know they were at the crime scene." Gibson looked at his list again. "There are only five houses on Lawsons Lane. We can visit everyone on the street without too much trouble. There were a number of people at the party. Let's see who we can narrow it down to. Until we identify that print, we have no suspects really."

"You mean like a needle in a haystack?"

He shrugged.

It was a clear route to bring them to Jonnie and Abigail Cunningham's home off Niagara Street. Eckhart parked against the curb, taking care not to rub the sides of her tires on the concrete. She didn't usually mind jumping the curb, but the lawn was too nice to mess with. The split-level house was set back off the street. They walked up the long driveway to the front door at the side of the house. An older Lincoln Continental, in a shade of blue hovering between midnight black and deep ocean sapphire that Gibson had never seen before, rested in the carport. They shuffled around it, cautious not to mark its pristine shine. He stood at the top of the stoop and rang the bell. The door was opened instantly by an older woman with curly blonde hair from a bottle, grey showing at the roots.

"Hello. May I help you?" Abigail asked.

The detectives flashed their badges.

"My husband's in the family room." She smiled and invited them in. They followed her down six steps of plush kiwi lime carpeting. A brick fireplace at the far wall had a wide cement mantel crammed with photographs from the last twenty-odd years. There was nobody around.

Abigail looked puzzled. "He was just here. Oh, maybe he went outside for a minute." She scurried away, her lips pressed into a concerned frown.

Gibson used the time to study the photos. One of a sailboat caught his attention, making him think about his kayak sitting in its rack at home. He drew in a heavy sigh. Eckhart plunked herself into a swivel chair next to the television, notebook fixed in her hand. The back-door latch rattled. A stout man clad in knee-length shorts and a golf shirt, ambled in, his wife bumping in behind. Her face looked more relaxed now.

"Here he is."

"Hello. Can my wife get you something to drink?" His double chin jiggled with a stifled laughter. Jonnie took his position on the couch where an indentation in the cushion marked his regular spot. His wife parked on the opposite side.

"No. We're good. Thank you. I'm Inspector Gibson and this is Inspector Eckhart. We have a few questions? First, are David and Jackie staying with you?"

"Yes, Jackie is our daughter. They live in BC," Abigail said.

"Are they around today?"

"They'll be back shortly." She looked at her husband for confirmation.

He nodded.

"Are Elsie and Jackie old friends?"

"Yes, but she was closer to Savannah, Elsie's sister. Then Jackie moved to BC. She only comes home once in a while. This time it was a special trip to see her dad. He's ill," Abigail said as if her husband wasn't in the room. She plucked at a hair on her chin and looked off.

Jonnie remained silent, sipping a brew he had abandoned beforehand.

"You both went to the fireworks." Not a question.

"Yes, we did." Abigail answered for both anyway.

"Did you know Elsie as well?"

"For ages. The whole family," Abigail said calmly, but her eyes betrayed her.

"Sorry for your loss." Gibson didn't know what else to say. He would be saying sorry to a lot of people. So far it seemed as if Elsie had plenty of friends but obviously one enemy as well.

Jonnie took another mouthful, draining the crystal tumbler. He held it up to his spouse. "Would you mind?"

"Okay." She grabbed his glass and turned to the detectives. "Sure you don't want anything?"

Gibson waved a hand in reply. She bustled to the kitchen, next floor up. The clinking of glass and a slammed cupboard door sailed down the stairs. She reappeared and arranged the drink on a coaster. Gibson let everyone settle back down before he continued.

"Did you see Elsie there? See her leave? Anything you noticed would be helpful."

"She was sitting with Jackie and Savannah, but she left before the fireworks started. That's pretty well all I know."

"What about you?" Gibson turned to her husband.

"She left right after the scuffle." He stirred his drink with a celery stick.

"What scuffle?" Gibson glanced at Eckhart. She shrugged.

"One of the young fellows from out of town and Anatoe."

"That's Jackie's second cousin removed. From Grimsby," Abigail added.

"He lives here now, dear."

"I know that. He has a garage. He fixes cars. Where is it again?" She peered at her husband.

"Down Niagara Street, close to town. Called Sinclair Motors."

"Anatoe Sinclair?" Gibson hazarded a wild guess. It was a name he knew from a long time ago. He looked down at the carpet and rubbed at his temple. The murder had happened before he had gotten a chance to find the person he was looking for—Cecilia Sinclair. Had it just fallen into his lap? Could he be that lucky? And what the hell did second cousin removed mean? That was Greek to him. But it was some kind of relative. It didn't matter.

"It was no biggy, just a boys-will-be-boys thing," Jonnie said.

"Oh, really? Who says that anymore? And not only that, but what about the name calling? Razing Elsie about her weight." She shook her head in disgust. "They're animals. The lot. That's what happens when you're brought up by a single mom."

"That's enough." Her husband spoke sharply.

Gibson glanced up somewhat surprised.

"Well, I don't admire any of them." She thumped her hand on the arm of the couch in finality and clamped her mouth shut, not wishing to get into a sparring match with her ill husband.

Gibson had stopped listening. Single mom. Yeah, it just fell into his lap—Cecilia. Had to be. His mind was going in a few directions at once. The bang brought him back to the room, and he stared into Abigail's eyes. They were a sepia brown with a ring of gold inside her iris that added a depth to her untold stories—if looks could kill. And she had just given him an unexpected tip-off to his own quandary. He heaved a sigh so deeply he thought everyone would question him, but nobody was paying any attention.

"Anything else you could tell us?" Gibson asked as if he was still in the moment.

"I don't think so." She shrugged.

Jonnie took another sip, but didn't say anything. It looked like tomato juice, but now Gibson figured it was mixed with beer.

A noise at the door alerted them to the arrival of the kids.

"Inspector, what are you doing here?" David asked. He stood at the top of the stairs.

"Hello, Mr. Hunter. I'm helping with the new Task Force. This is Inspector Eckhart."

Gibson felt a presence behind him and swung around. Jackie stood in the doorway of the back door. Her eyes scanned the room and met his smoky grey eyes.

"Hello, Jackie."

"Hi. This is weird." She gave a quick bark of laughter.

They both entered the room and took seats by the fireplace.

"As I said to David, I'm on a special assignment. Nice to see you." Then he got down to business.

"Let's start at the fireworks and work our way from there. Tell me what you know. Go ahead, David."

"Well, I was sitting with Jackie, Savannah and Elsie. Some guy came over, but Elsie told him to take a hike. There was a small scuffle at the far end of the field that didn't amount to anything." David paused. "A little later, some guys were calling Elsie names again. You know, fat jokes. I think she was embarrassed because she left shortly after." A blonde lock of hair slipped over his right eye. He nudged it back.

Gibson waited.

"When I went out to the road to stretch my legs, I heard some yelling down by the landing. Two people. One of them was Elsie for sure."

Gibson leaned into David.

"Who was with her?"

"I can't be certain, but I think it was the guy that does that thing with his eye. The one that Elsie had already yelled at. It was dark. There aren't any street lights on the lane."

"That's my cousin, Anatoe," Jackie said. "I didn't see him talking to Elsie. Where was that?"

"At the fireworks. You were too busy talking to Savannah. Anyway, I'm not sure it was him or not. I couldn't actually see his face." He hesitated. "But it was the way he moved that made me think it was him."

Gibson stole a peek at Eckhart.

"What were they quarreling about?"

"I don't know. I couldn't make out what they were saying, but I think it was something about Savannah." He shrugged. "Next thing they were both gone."

Gibson thought it sounded like Anatoe was being a nuisance. Or was he more than just a pest? A killer? If it was Anatoe at all.

"Give me a rundown on what you saw Jackie."

"Wait."

Gibson looked over to David.

"There was someone else there."

"Who?" Gibson leaned in further.

"Mr. Tatlow. I've seen him once before. You know the creepy guy?" David hadn't wanted to say anything because Jackie and her friends kept saying he was a monster from way back when. That might make Tatlow a target. They might railroad the guy and he wasn't even sure it was him. "I shouldn't have said anything. I knew it."

"It's okay. We'll check it out." He saw Eckhart doodling in her notebook. Probably a couple of giant question marks. "What about you, Jackie?"

"I didn't notice anything except Elsie leaving. I hadn't seen Savannah for years, so I was wrapped up in all the gossip." She paused. "The news." She shrugged in apology.

"Now, let's move on. How did you happen to be on the beach?" He turned back to David.

"We actually never made it to the beach. Well we did, but not like you think." He stopped, his tongue tied into a knot. "Let me start from the beginning. Jackie and I were headed for the beach, but Gregory came tearing up the stairs. He said Elsie was dead and just ran off. We tried to stop him. Jackie and I went down to see…" David stopped.

"It's all right. I know, it's hard."

"I saw Elsie face down in the sand. All I could do was stare. Her body didn't look right. I knew she was dead even before I checked her pulse. Then I called 911."

Jackie's bronze skin had a pale hue to it as if she was going to faint.

"I understand that Todd showed up. What happened?" Gibson hoped he would get some clarity about what the husband had done down on the beach.

"We were waiting on the landing. Todd ran down to the beach, so I ran after him. He didn't touch anything. I'll swear to that. I knew that would be important. You know, from the last time…"

"Go on."

"Then the cops came. They asked a bunch of questions and we left."

It was good that Todd hadn't touched anything, Gibson thought. Not while David was there anyway. This could be crucial later when they got the print off the rock. He glanced over to Eckhart and saw her scribbling in the notebook. Yeah, she'd got that written down.

"Savannah was there too," Jackie said, "but she didn't go down to the beach."

"So the four of you went to Todd's house after. Is that correct?"

"Yeah. Jackie and I stayed the night. To make sure Todd and Savannah would be okay." He shook his head. "That's a joke."

"Thanks for your help. Call if you remember anything else. No matter how small it may seem. You've been through this before, so you know."

David nodded that he understood, although his complexion had turned almost as white as his wife's.

"Sorry for your loss, Jackie. I know you have been friends for a long time."

"Thanks." Her voice cracked.

"We'll see ourselves out." Gibson stood up and motioned to his partner.

"Take care." Eckhart shoved her notebook into a pocket and also stood.

Abigail walked them out.

"You'll find out who did this?"

"We're trying our best."

"Thanks." Her lashes were laden with moisture.

"They didn't have anything to do with the murder," Eckhart said as they walked to the truck.

"No."

As they were walking down the drive, Gibson glanced backwards. Abigail waved from the bay window. Eckhart drove down the street and cleared the corner.

"Okay. How about a nightcap tonight?" She ran her tongue over her plump lips.

His smoky eyes followed the movement.

"Sure."

Eckhart bit her lip and a sudden pink blushed her cheeks. She smiled in that way that he had seen in a movie—shy and demure.

Gazing straight ahead, Gibson wasn't sure which direction they were going, but soon they passed his motel room. The small bridge to Port Dalhousie came up next. It was a beautiful spot where the lake could be seen when looking down almost any street. Eckhart took a few side roads and then finally pulled into a paved driveway quite near to the water.

The upscale Brownstone townhouse was an end unit of six. They headed up a flight of stone steps to a crimson door with hanging baskets on either side in front of side glass panels. The foyer was minimalist with a long teak table along one wall. A huge mirror in a thin pewter frame was centred on top. The hardwood floors started at the front door and covered every square inch, all in a deep chocolate hue. From where Gibson stood, he could look into the living room and out the large windows to the lake in the north. The open concept kitchen was over to the right. The bedrooms were hidden down another long hallway on the left.

"Wow. That's a nice view."

"Isn't it though?" Eckhart took his hand and led him to the couch. "Have a seat while I get us a drink. A nice pinot gris from the peninsula?"

"That sounds perfect." Gibson sat facing the vista and wondered if he was ready to take the dip into the unknown. The couch was soft under his fingertips—exquisite buttercup yellow leather. Several creamy coloured armchairs faced a gas fireplace with a small flat screen above. There were a few original oil paintings hanging on one of the lengthy walls—red, blues and yellow in an abstract style. A scattering of oriental rugs broke up the dark of the hardwood and gave the space a comfy feeling. He stood up and walked to the window, looking down into the yard. The garden was tame with climbing roses at the back fence and an assortment of shrubs.

"Do you like?" Eckhart whispered in his ear.

Gibson turned around and stood inches from her, his primal desire stirred. He drew her into him and kissed her full on, open-mouthed, her lips trembling under his. The world fell away. They pulled apart and stared at each other—pale smoke to deep ocean blue.

"I should go." The water was too hot.

Chapter 6

The air had grown even heavier with a stifling humidity. Gibson breathed in deeply, sniffing the heady essence of rain. A stony grey belt on the horizon marred the velvet sky. A lazy breeze dragged the clouds across the lake.

The café was full today. A couple stood up to leave, so Gibson snagged their place by the window. He had an hour to burn and ordered breakfast. A large woman swept by and jarred the table. The scalding coffee spilt over his hand. He yanked aside, holding his cell in the air. The liquid rolled along the surface and dripped to the floor just missing his pant leg. She looked at him with disdain and nudged her course down the aisle. He scooted out of the way as the waitress mopped the puddle.

"Sorry."

"No problem. Wasn't your fault." She moved away, staring down the plump older woman.

Gibson eased back into his chair, simmering over his actions the day before. Why hadn't he called Katherine last night? She needed to know he was ensnared in a homicide case. Was he entangled in more? He rocked his skull, rattled his brain. What was going on with him? His glance darted to the other patrons as if they knew his inner turmoil. Had he cheated on her yet? Not really. It was just a kiss. He placed his fingers to his mouth. Well, not just a kiss. It was passionate. When he had leaned into her body, it had the perfect blend of serenity and tension. He couldn't phone Katherine. His voice would give him away. He looked at his cell and cheated again, in a different way. He sent her a text and shut down his phone.

The SUV snuck around the corner and sidled up to the curb. Eckhart's gaze through the plate-glass window was subtle, her eyebrows narrowed. He flipped a coin on the table for a tip and walked out the door.

"Hi. Have a nice sleep?" Her sultry voice caressed his face.

"Feels like rain is coming." He skirted the question because all he had dreamt about was her.

"I think you're right," she said.

"Okay. The first house nearest the beach landing is Felton and Margaret Cunningham's place. Felton is Jonnie's older brother. Jackie's uncle. That's where the fireworks and party were anyway."

He took a quick glance at his notes.

"The house on the left coming up the steps. That's the same address as Gregory. Must be their son," he continued.

"That's handy."

* * *

Felton's lot was five acres of flat pasture. At the rear, a section of native plants severed his land from the neighbours. The left boundary rose into a bank that dropped down to the shore below. A tall hedge on the right closed off access to the house next door, except for a tiny hidden opening that someone could scoot through, if they knew it was there. The Expedition ground to a standstill in the driveway sending dust into the air. A newly painted hut near the road sported a fresh roof. Farther along, the open gate of the potting shed showed neatly stacked tools and a bench. The gardens appeared tended with an exceptionally nice exhibit of dahlias.

The two-storey clapboard house seemed tired compared to the outbuildings with its peeling paint of a nondescript shade, perhaps a blue. A traditional veranda with rustic wooden scrolling stretched across the full facade. The steps leading up were broad and welcoming. Two wicker armchairs with floral cushions hugged a wrought-iron table. A mug stood empty on its glass surface. Someone had tossed a pair of well-worn garden gloves and a straw hat onto an ottoman.

Down at the far end of the porch, a swing bench hung from a thick, rusted chain. A hedgehog boot scraper waited by the screen entry. Margaret stood in the doorway, an amiable smile on her fat face, the dark mole on her snout quite prominent. Her Brillo Pad hair was mousy brown overgrown with grey. Dingy sweatpants smeared with soil on the thighs were pulled up over her ample belly. The gingham blouse was a pinpoint of colour in her shabby appearance, like a blossom in a weed patch.

"You must be the detectives?"

He looked up. Really. How do they always know? He looked back at the logo on the passenger door. Right, it was an official vehicle. Not like his at home where he drove incognito in his own truck.

"Inspector Gibson." He pointed to his partner. "Inspector Eckhart."

"Come in. Are you thirsty? I have fresh lemonade."

"That sounds good. Thank you." Gibson wiped his brow. "I haven't been in this kind of hot weather for a while."

"Oh?"

"I live in BC now. Just helping set up the Task Force here."

"That's nice."

They followed Margaret to the rear of the house, her clogs clomping on the tired pine floor in the hallway.

Bright light slanted through the windows into the kitchen. The enormous room boasted appliances from the forties. Or where they retro? No. He noticed several chips on the edge of the cooker. Definitely old. He perched on a wooden stool and grappled to get comfortable, launching a dart over to Eckhart. She concealed her face to cut off a laugh and alighted on the only cushioned chair around the table. Margaret poured two generous glasses.

"Good stuff." The drink ran down his parched throat smoothly and soothed his fiery mouth.

"It's the well water," Margaret said.

"Honestly. No water line down this road?"

"There is, but we prefer the pure taste." She hesitated and peered toward the hallway. "Right, Felton?"

"Yeah, yeah." A thin rack of a man hobbled into the gallery and rested at the head of the table, scraping his chair all along the linoleum. He inhaled a quick snort of air with a load of phlegm that sent him into a barking cough. It shifted into a fit of wheezing and hacking. He pulled out a handkerchief and spat. A small puff of smoke came out of his mouth. He rolled his tongue, sticking it out as if he was struggling to dislodge an object trapped in his teeth. The stench of burnt tobacco permeated the room.

Eckhart wiggled her nose.

"Felton, this is Gibson and Eckhart from the police."

Close enough Gibson thought.

"We have a few questions."

"About the accident? We don't know anything about that," Felton said.

"It wasn't an accident. Someone murdered Elsie," Gibson said.

"What! I thought it was an accident," Margaret shouted and plopped down into a chair.

Felton grabbed a cigarette.

"Outside with that, Felton."

"Ah, never mind." He sat back, crossed his arms and grunted.

"Who was at your party?"

"Lots of people. Anatoe and his Grimsby friends. Felton's younger brother from town with his troop."

"That's Jackie's dad, right?" Cunningham. He got the connection.

"Yeah."

"What about Gregory? He found the body."

"I didn't see him or his bike," Margaret answered. Her eyes had narrowed, the pleasantness in her voice knocked down to toleration. "He's a good boy. He put a new roof on the pumphouse at the front. And he's painting the house for us."

"Is he around now? We need to speak to him as well." Gibson had only seen one car out front, but he had to ask anyway.

"No. He went out early this morning." Her eyes changed into slits.

"Did you see Elsie?"

"She was sitting with her sister, Savannah, and I guess that was Jackie with her, my niece. I thought she moved out west."

"Did you see Elsie leave?"

"No."

"Any idea why she would leave early?"

"Not really. No reason for me to know." Margaret paused. "Maybe to check up on Todd."

"What do you mean?"

"He keeps the store open until closing time no matter what. So I suppose he was still counting cash or something."

"So, she might have been heading there?"

Margaret shrugged.

Yeah, except Elsie went the other way toward the beach. Was she meeting someone? Gibson wondered.

"What were you doing all that time?" he asked.

"I was helping Felton. Getting the guys beer and stuff."

"Did you see anybody?" He turned to Felton.

"Too busy with the fireworks."

"Who were the men helping you?" Gibson asked.

"Some friends." He glared at the detective and gave Eckhart a sideways glance, admiring her good looks like most men did. Gibson waited.

"A guy I met at the bar a few years ago. And his son." He coughed into his handkerchief again and cleared his throat. "They live in a trailer park by the canal."

"Could we have names?"

Eckhart poised her hand over the notepad and wrote down the info.

"What about the store? Will they close it?" Margaret asked.

"For now, I'm sure," Gibson said and pulled at his sweat drenched collar.

"It's muggy enough to rain. I can feel it coming," Margaret said, nodding with authority.

Eckhart sat quietly.

"Okay. Thanks for your time."

"All right, officer."

Felton ignored them.

The detectives headed down the hallway, Margaret pursuing close behind.

Gibson cast a backward look as they drove off. Ominous clouds shoved each other in the northeastern sky. They tumbled into larger foreboding masses as they raced across the lake on a wind Gibson couldn't feel.

"Yikes. We're in for trouble."

Chapter 7

"What should we do?" Jackie asked.

"We better go see how Todd and Savannah are doing," David answered.

The tires hummed along the sticky tarmac, changing to a low purr when they hit the metal grid of the bridge. Jackie looked down the canal and gathered in a breath. A familiar friend in this hostile world. The essence of earthy loam from the lushness all around seeped into the car vents. A reminder of long summer days and wasted youth. She lowered her eyes and inclined her head backward.

Jacobs Landing. No light glowed from within. It appeared deserted, shutters sealed to life. Flowers in the terracotta pots were limp beyond promise. David felt as wilted as the flowers. He was feeling the soaring temperatures more than his wife. They trudged down the narrow stone pathway, holding hands tightly. The one-storey house had a gabled roof and dark wood-framed windows. The porch had little embellishment except for the intricate wrought-iron railing. He knocked, paused and waited for a response, and tapped again. Savannah swung open the door. A huge yawn, splotchy skin and bloodshot eyes suggested sleep deprivation. She tugged at her greasy hair.

"Is Todd awake?" David asked.

"He's in the kitchen. Better come in."

Heat punched them from behind, trying to invade the house. Savannah crossed her arms over her chest as if a chill had hit her. David hastened to the rear of the house, leaving the women standing in the foyer.

"Let's go to the beach," Jackie said.

"I guess," Savannah answered.

They ambled down the dusty lane, Grandma's home on the right, the Underwood family residence on the left. A long tract of meadow grasses played in the faint breeze as they lumbered along. Past the fields, Felton's place came into view. Below the bluff across the street, barely visible stood a house tucked behind a row of trees and native shrubbery. The neighbourhood bogeyman lived there— Mr. Hugh Tatlow. Jackie had seen him the other day, and he had looked the same as she had remembered him—a giant guy with black eyes and a piercing glare. Creepy. As a kid, she had invariably eluded his property and ran like hell if she encountered him.

Savannah faltered on the beach landing, inhaled a breath and risked the first step. She skirted the depression at the bottom. The coast swept away into the distance, fading at a curve. As if drawn by a magnet, the girls wended their way to the lake, hot sand shifting under their feet. The water was chilly in contrast. Savannah wiggled her toes as the silvery bubbling crests curled past her naked limbs to strike the shoreline with softness. Overhead the sunlight pulsed down from a pastel blue sky. The seagulls screamed and whirled gracefully with the thermals.

They found a shaded patch against the dunes where timbers had sailed in from winter storms. The driftwood bleached by the summer rays sat pale in their current home until the next squall reclaimed them. Jackie pushed backward into an arched hollow on an auspicious log. She passed her fingers over the ridges that swirled along its surface. She was undecided what to say to her grieving companion. Savannah remained quietly beside her. The melody of the wash licking the sand made it tough for Jackie to hold her eyes open. The sun stabbed a tunnel through the shivering leaves and touched down on Savannah's fiery red hair. The same ruby hue as Elsie's locks. Jackie's moan of sadness was not lost upon her friend.

The restless night had weighed on Jackie's resilience, and she nodded off. The squealing of gulls startled her from her nap. Savannah was gone. She felt alone. A sharp wind sent goosebumps along her arms. She glanced up at the black clouds hurrying in and sprawling across the sky. A brilliant force of lightning shocked her to her feet. A boom made her jump. The squall unleashed itself, lashing the top of the water, hurling spray into the air. Drops of rain changed into casks as she tripped up the stairs. Each lightning crack and rumble of thunder sounding closer. When she reached the landing, a flash lit up all around. The detonation came moments afterward. Jackie rushed forward from peril straight into the arms of a stranger. She hollered, wrenching herself loose from his powerful grasp. Black evil eyes glared at Jackie, making her run as fast as she could. She careened down the lane, tears cascading down her cheeks. A hand captured her. She screeched wildly, and whirled round to face her fear.

* * *

Todd had gone back to bed, so David wandered outside to the store. He stood on the stoop with a lit smoke, staring at the gathering storm. The sky had dimmed, but the heat hadn't let up. The clouds bunched together closer, blacker and steeper. A spark of lightning split the sky, and a deafening boom crackled overhead. He butted out his fag and decided to look for the girls. As he headed down the roadway more forks of lightning and thunder rolled over him. The clouds broke free and dumped rain onto his hurrying figure. An Expedition whipped out of Grandma's driveway almost colliding into him. He continued moving quicker, his limbs working overtime until he spotted Jackie. She was running blindly down the lane with her eyes lowered. He grabbed at her arm to slow her down. She struggled to get away.

"It's me."

She looked up and fell into his body.

"Mr. Tatlow. He tried to…"

"It's okay. Let's get out of this downpour," David assured her.

Chapter 8

"Who's next on our list?" Gibson studied the list. His finger paused at Mrs. Mary Cunningham. "We'll visit Grandma. If it's at all like my family, people will just show up. Maybe Gregory is there."

Grandma's home was adjacent to the roadway. The two-storey white building had an expansive wraparound veranda on both levels. It was the perfect grandchild playground. Lots of space to run and bike. Apple trees, their gnarled branches weighted with fruit spurs, peppered the grassland on the right. Jacobs Landing stood out across the field. The hedge on the left blocked out Felton's dwelling.

There were rose beds here and there about the house and along the driveway. Lavender and marigolds weaved in with the shrubs. Katherine would treasure this, Gibson thought. He shut his eyes for a flash and sighed. Grandma rested in a rocker by the front door, hands on lap, gazing at the darkness rolling in. Bobby pins, stuck in randomly, barely kept the puffs of silvery hair in control. Her skin was weathered and wrinkly.

"Good afternoon," Gibson said as he walked to the porch.

"Are you the detectives?"

"Yes. May we ask a few questions?"

"What a dreadful affair. Poor Elsie."

Eckhart picked a basket weave chair opposite the elderly woman and sat. Gibson leaned on the railing and crossed his arms.

"Would you like some water? Not as good as Felton's. But it's icy." The rocker groaned as she broke its motion with feet stuck on the ground. She reached for the glass beside her.

He shook his head and smirked at the dig directed at Felton and his well water.

"Did you notice anything at the party? Anybody follow Elsie out or anything?" Gibson asked, figuring Grandma didn't miss much.

"I'm not so young anymore. I went home before the fireworks started. I really can't help you." Her head had bobbed up and down as she listened, her mouth twisted into a frown.

A pickup ripped into the entrance and came to a halt with a skid in the dirt. It was a classic 1950s Chevrolet, a no-expense spared restoration with an awesome turquoise paint job that popped.

"There's B… Anatoe," Grandma said. She had almost called him by his nickname, Blinkers, but thought better of it.

A long-limbed man in his early thirties hopped out and walked by the Expedition, glancing at the official logo on the door. A crooked smile quickly flashed and retired. He sauntered up to the stoop and set a foot on the lower tread. Grease stained his coveralls and encrusted his palms. He stood as tall as Gibson. He had beefy square shoulders and a tense square jaw with earthy brown eyes, a spark of soul showing and a wariness hiding behind. He was a dead ringer for the lady Gibson had known so well long ago. Gibson looked at the ground and rubbed at his face.

"Just checking up on you," Anatoe said and smiled at Gran. Not his grandmother, but it felt like it.

"I'm fine. These are the police."

"Hey." He remained on the bottom step and placed his hands on his hips.

"I understand you run a repair shop," Gibson said.

"Yeah." His eye ticked ever so slightly.

"Nice truck. Did you fix it up yourself?"

"Yeah." Anatoe stared at Eckhart.

"Someone murdered Elsie," Grandma blurted out. Anatoe took his gaze from the inspector and looked at Grandma instead.

"Huh. I thought she tumbled down the stairs." His glance bounced toward Gibson.

"I'm afraid it wasn't an accident. Did you see anything?" Gibson said.

"What? I don't know anything."

A flash ripped in the eastern sky. A crack in the air followed closely. The thunder rolled across the blue-steel grey expanse like a non-stop train. Gibson raised his gaze to black clouds sweeping in quickly. The next strike of lightening hit moments afterward. Another explosion sounded near to where they stood, the rumbling echoing off the lake.

"What about the fight?"

"It was nothing. That was just some jerks being nasty to Elsie. I tried to straighten them out. She didn't deserve that."

"Where did you go after that?"

"I went over to the fireworks pit. Then I grabbed a beer from the house."

"Did anyone see you in your wanderings?" Gibson asked.

"I don't know. They were all busy getting things set up."

"David saw you arguing with Elsie on the landing."

"That's ridiculous. Wasn't me. He's mistaken me for someone else," Anatoe said.

Gibson hoped that was true. Besides, David didn't seem clear about what he saw. He took a photo of the ring out of his pocket and handed it over. "Are you part of this fraternity?"

"Yeah, Alpha Zee."

"Where's your ring?" Gibson rubbed at his finger.

"I gave it to a lady last year." He grimaced. "Never got it back after we split."

"Who are the members?"

"Just a few guys from Grimsby."

"Have names for us?"

"Sure. No problem," Anatoe said.

Eckhart wrote as he called out the individuals.

"Anything else you can add?"

He shrugged a shoulder.

The next brilliant zigzag of light crashed down by the shore almost simultaneously with a crackle of thunder. A patter of raindrops fell and then lashed down in torrential sheets. Anatoe bounded up the stairs to avoid getting drenched. Gibson moved away from the railing. Tree boughs swayed and groaned in the sudden gale.

"Thanks for your help." Gibson shot a glance toward Eckhart. He bounded off the porch and made a mad dash for the truck.

"Let's hunt down Felton's firework buddies," Gibson said.

"Okay." Eckhart drew her pad from a pocket and flipped through it, searching for an address. She tapped the page. "They live by the canal. On this side. I know the place."

He nodded.

"Should we grab a quick bite before we go?"

"Good idea."

As Eckhart turned into the first market she encountered, the rain stopped as quickly as it had started.

That was pretty typical for this part of the world in the summer.

There were plenty of bins of fresh local fruits and vegetables. Looked promising. They grabbed a couple of cold drinks and sandwiches from the cooler. Gibson bit down on his tuna sandwich and stopped mid chomp. It hadn't been his first choice of fillings, but there hadn't been much selection. He swung to his partner and saw she had the same look on her face. He tossed most of his lunch into a bin just outside the entrance of the store.

"Yuck. Definitely not the Mansion Pub," he spat.

"Touché." She followed suit and pitched her sandwich in the garbage.

They headed to a service road that ran parallel to the canal. A wire fence circled the trailer park. Eckhart drove down the muddy track between rows of mobile homes. The truck bounced in the wide ruts. They discovered the place they were seeking at the top of the second row, just as Felton described it. A hoarder's paradise. Junk filled the meager lot in front: a sink, some irrigation pipe and a jumble of tangled metal. An old fridge stood vacant at the side of the mobile home, accompanied by a rusted-out water tank. A tarp attached to the flimsy aluminium wall flapped in the breeze. The whole yard looked like a fire risk. He glanced at the neighbour's garden. It was respectable, even had a wooden tub of geraniums.

Gibson had run both their names through the system with the equipment in the Expedition. The father was clean, but the kid had a possession charge from three years ago. It didn't matter anymore though, because weed was now legal in Canada. He thought he'd never see the day. He shook his head.

The structure rattled when Gibson tapped on the door.

"Yeah, what do you want?"

"It's the police."

May as well keep it simple. A chair scraped along the floor, and heavy footsteps caused the trailer to shake. An old man in a greasy plaid shirt with jeans that hung below his waistline stood in the entrance. He hiked them up, hauling on the frayed belt.

"Nothing to say to the police," the old man said.

"Don't worry. We just want to ask a few questions about the fireworks."

"At Felton's house?"

"Yes."

Some banging reverberated from the back.

"Is that your son?"

"Get over here," the old man whooped. A scruffy looking individual came around the corner and froze when he spotted the detectives.

"What?" the kid snapped, jutting out his jaw.

"They want to know about the fireworks."

"What about them?" The kid forced his lips together into a scowl, and made an offensive gesture with his yellowed fingers, gunk under his broken nails.

"You were both helping?"

The old man nodded. The kid lowered his angry eyebrows.

"Who was there besides Felton?"

"Margaret. She served us cold beers," the old man replied. Not quite as belligerent as his offspring.

"That's right," the kid said. The tone of his voice revealing his dislike of cops.

"Did Felton leave the site at all?"

"Just to take a piss," the kid said, laughing so hard he doubled over at his own joke, almost pissing his own pants with the effort.

"Did you see anybody else?"

"Anatoe came round. Said hi and went in the house for a beer. He never came back. Then we lit the fireworks. That's it."

"I'm kind of busy. Can I go now?" the kid asked.

"Thanks for your cooperation."

The kid spat on the ground and stalked off. The old man offered a half-hearted shrug.

They hopped into the truck. Eckhart steered through the park, dodging children playing in the muck. She pulled into a narrow path off the main road, the bumper pushing through the unmown grass. Gibson had a pretty good idea where she was headed.

"Have you been here before?" she asked and pulled to a stop in a small clearing overlooking the canal.

"Yes. It's been quite a while."

Eckhart stepped out and leaned on the hood. Gibson got out and stood in front of her. He brushed her hair back from her shoulders and nuzzled her neck, inhaling the sweet scent of her perfume. The kiss was hot, fiery and passionate. He could feel the beating of her heart against his chest. He stopped and looked into her eyes. Their fingers grazed as he moved away. He knew it was just a matter of time before it happened, but not today. She stayed where she was for a moment, turning to look at him through the windshield. Then she returned to the chill of the truck and started up the engine.

"That rain sure cooled things down." Eckhart sucked her lips in.

"Yeah." That was a clever reply, Gibson thought. His mind was doing flip flops.

She fiddled with the radio knob until she found a soft rock station playing a song by a local group that had made it big. The silence between them was effortless and pleasant. He settled into his seat and looked out the window. Clouds drifted across the sky with the gentle breeze. Aspen trees bordered the service road that ran alongside the canal. Their quivering leaves intercepted the sunlight periodically. Two ships met and passed each other. One rose high in the water. It would be empty, heading back to the St. Lawrence River and to places remote. The other one was heavy, fully loaded. Small waves licked the Plimsoll line stamped on the hull. He speculated what the payload was. He closed his eyes, sensing Eckhart peeking over to him. At the motel, she threw the gears into park and turned to him.

"I—"

"Pick me up at eight? Same place?" He grabbed her hand and squeezed.

"You bet." She gave him a demure smile.

* * *

After a dinner alone in the motel restaurant, Gibson went back to his suite to unwind. He settled on top of the tousled bed sheets fresh from a shower. He was intoxicated with a sense of freedom that he had never felt with Katherine. Was it real? He had been tempted to jump in and find out, but—the fact that there was a but had stopped him. His cell chirped. It was Scottie, Sergeant Cruickshank, his partner in Victoria.

"Hey, I was just going to phone."

"Sure." Her laughter reverberated through the line and overflowed into the dreary room. Like birdsong, it created brightness.

"No, really." He sat up, fluffed the pillow and melted into its softness. He spread his limbs out and crisscrossed them at the ankles.

"Will you be back by the weekend? You thought—"

"No," he answered quickly.

"Oh, matters aren't progressing smoothly then."

"The worst. A homicide was thrust onto the Task Force, and the unit isn't set up properly yet."

"Yikes. So, what are you looking at?"

"I suppose I'm here for at least another week," he said. "How's it going there?"

"Nothing exciting happening here. Just catching up on some reports." Scottie paused. The tone of his voice made her curious. "Have you spoken to Katherine?"

"Yes." The lie slipped out fast and easy.

"She'll be fine," Scottie said, her voice equivocal.

"I'm sure. Got to go. I'll call again soon."

"Guess what, Billy? I phoned you."

The giggle was ear splitting this time. He yanked the cell from his skull. Why did she persist with that nickname?

"All right. See you."

His phone chirped as soon as he hung up. He looked at the screen and groaned. It was the call he feared. Should he answer? Of course. He had to. No. He would let it go to voice mail. Collect himself and call back. Coward.

"Hi, sweetheart." He answered on the seventh ring.

"Hello." Katherine's pitch was charming with a hint of amusement. "Only three more days."

Gibson studied the print on the wall, a hotchpotch of colours. A meadow? Flowers? After merely a moment's hesitation, he announced in his most dismal voice, "I'm trapped here longer than expected. There's been a murder."

"What? You can't. It's not your problem." Her tone drew tight with controlled irritation.

"They're counting on me. You don't miss me anyway," he said in his dreamiest voice.

"I do miss you." Her intonation thawed. "I suppose it's okay. I am awfully busy."

"What's up?" he asked, immediately suspicious, his guilt playing at the back of his mind.

"I have interviews."

"Oh." He relaxed and slumped heavier into the bed.

"Yeah, wish me luck."

"You'll get the perfect job. Don't you fret."

"Okay. Talk to you later." Katherine disconnected the call before he could respond.

That was a first. Usually she dragged the conversation on, refusing to disengage. He closed his eyes and descended into an uneasy slumber.

Chapter 9

Gibson woke up early, leaped out of bed and rolled his neck back and forth making it crack. He got ready to face the day and stepped outside to a splendid morning. The deluge had turned the thermometer down. He relaxed at the same table in Just Roasted Cafe and ordered a coffee and a toasted bagel with cheese. After his second cup, he glanced at his watch. The Expedition showed up soon after. Eckhart greeted him with a gentle smile.

He jumped into the vehicle and settled into the soft leather. Two sheets of paper were balanced on the centre console. He glanced at Eckhart.

"Not a lot of detail. It's just the basics. The top one is about Mr. Hugh Tatlow."

"Anything out of the ordinary?" Gibson asked as he glanced at the page.

"He was in the armed forces. A career man."

"Married?"

"Yes, but his wife died. And the baby too."

"Whoa. That's brutal." Gibson thought about Katherine's miscarriage with her ex-husband. Not entirely the same, but still. He picked up the second sheet. Plenty of tragedy lived on Lawsons Lane.

"Should we go to the station first?" Eckhart asked.

"Let me call Frenchy," Gibson replied. He punched in the lab number and waited. She didn't answer. He cradled his cell in his palm. "What do—" A chirp interrupted him.

"Gibson."

"I was in the midst of something," Frenchy said.

"That's okay. Any news about the prints?"

"I can't lift them yet."

"Okay. What about the software program?"

"My guy is still working on it. Uncertain what the issue is, but..."

"Okay, Frenchy."

"Don't worry. It'll happen." She hung up without waiting for a retort.

"Nothing new."

"I figured that," Eckhart said. She inclined into the bucket seat and glimpsed at the wispy clouds gliding along peacefully, non-threatening. She looked down the road, her thoughts wandering elsewhere.

"So, Lawsons Lane?" Gibson asked.

"Okay."

The trip down the lane wasn't dusty this time, but a light wind was kicking up from the lake. Eckhart cruised to the end, swinging into the last entrance. The house loomed up ahead. It was a grand two-storey Queen Anne Revival building with a turret at the front corner overlooking the lake. The hipped roof with cross-gables reached toward the sky. Elaborate fish scale siding covered nearly the entire exterior facade. Several windows on the lower level had stained glass. A sweep of steps led to a veranda with lacy spindles adorning the posts and railings.

Gibson punched the bell. A melodic song rang out. The door was opened by a broad man with grizzled hair. His brown eyes were kind with a hint of sorrow on the margins. Not as creepy as the kids made out. The furrows etched on his features supported his tragedy—a profound loss. The lines softened when he smiled.

"It's about Elsie," he said, gesturing them into the formal vestibule.

The walls were embossed with velour to the wainscoting. Someone had created mahogany built-ins. The parquet flooring was polished to a mirror finish.

"This is a lovely house," Gibson said.

"I bought it for my partner and..."

"Sorry for your loss."

"It was a long time ago," he said and flapped it off with a toss of his hand.

Nevertheless, it still hurt, Gibson guessed.

"I expect you heard that Elsie was murdered. It wasn't an accident."

"Mary mentioned it. Across the lane."

Grandma.

"Did you see anything?" Gibson asked.

"I was returning from my nightly stroll when the fireworks started."

"From the beach?"

"No. Down the street and back." He paused. "I was hiking up my drive when I overheard some squabbling. It was Elsie and Anatoe."

"Did you hear what they were talking about?" Now we know it was Anatoe for sure, Gibson thought. He glanced at his partner. She smirked.

"Something about Savannah. It was none of my business."

Gibson waited. Eckhart scratched in her journal.

"They both left. Not sure who went where. I saw another fellow come along, but he split right away."

That would have been David.

"That's all I can report. If I had realized..." Mr. Tatlow sighed.

"How could you have possibly known what was going to happen?" Gibson said, his soft intonation giving the man some solace.

Mr. Tatlow made a noise of acknowledgement.

"Thanks for your help. We may talk to you again."

Gibson walked down the drive, suddenly aware that the wind had dropped altogether. They hopped into the truck and headed down the lane.

* * *

"The Underwoods lost their only child ten years ago. Katie. Apparently, she drowned. What a shame." He fingered the paper.

Eckhart spun into the next driveway. It was an ordinary clapboard dwelling as divergent from Mr. Tatlow's place as day to night. Large trees loomed over the yard and heavily shaded the lawn. The gardens were pleasing with bundles of annual colour. Climbing roses on the face of the house blossomed in a rich pink blush. The front entrance didn't have a portico and stood open to the weather. There were no fancy scrolling or railings on the scant landing. Chairs dotted the grass in groups, for the most part in the shade. He knocked on the door. Mrs. Underwood answered, glancing at the emblem on their vehicle.

"Hello. Come in." She signaled them to the living room. All the furnishings were spotless and tasteful. The essence of spices wafted from the rear. "It's the detectives."

"Coffee?" Mr. Underwood rose from his loveseat and gestured to a couch by the window. He sat back down.

"That would be nice," Gibson said. He sat and looked out the window toward Grandma's house. Eckhart perched next to him.

"I won't be a moment. Bear with me." Mrs. Underwood scurried down the hallway, soft footfalls resounding in the small space.

"She's an excellent cook."

Gibson smiled. Eckhart reached for her journal, ready to take notes.

Mrs. Underwood came back with a big tray. "I have sandwiches too." She arranged the works on a table between the two seating arrangements. After everybody was established with a plate of food and steaming coffee, she sank into the loveseat. The couple remained close but not touching, linked by a force that flowed between them.

"Did you make it to the fireworks?" Gibson asked.

"No. We didn't go," Mr. Underwood said.

"It was ten years ago to the date we lost our child," his wife said matter-of-factly.

Although he was aware of the story, Gibson felt his heart strike his rib cage.

"Katie had gone out on her bike with friends. A day like today. Perfect." Mrs. Underwood inhaled sharply and went on. "She was with Savannah from the store. Jackie was at her grandma's house that weekend, as well." She pointed across the street.

Gibson's heart darted around his chest, seeking for a place to stash his emotions. Eckhart sat straight, mouth drawn. It was painful to listen to Mrs. Underwood speak in such a neutral manner.

"I presume the girls separated. I discovered Katie's bike at the top of the beach stairs. The police suggested she had drowned." She shrugged. "We never recovered her body. What could we do?"

The detectives sat still.

"It's okay. We're okay." She reached over the coffee table and touched Gibson's sleeve. He was reluctant to look her in the eye. When he did, he didn't see the emptiness he was expecting, but hope—hope that Katie was at peace. His heart settled into its appointed spot.

Mrs. Underwood squeezed his arm and smiled a smile that brought memories back. Gibson swallowed hard. This was what heartbreak felt like. He had experienced it once before when his younger brother had committed suicide. A tear threatened to expose him. "I'm so sorry for your loss." He perched on the brink of the couch.

Mrs. Underwood glanced skyward and exhaled. Mr. Underwood patted her hand.

"Thank you for your time." He pointed a chin at Eckhart and rose. "And the snacks."

Gibson wasn't certain what he was feeling when they left. Despair? Hope? Guilt?

Eckhart looked distressed.

"Late lunch?" he asked.

"Yeah. How about the Mansion Pub? I love their Reuben sandwich."

Eckhart fired up the engine. The drive downtown was quick. The traffic had thinned considerably. She discounted the 'No Parking' sign in front of the pub and parked with the truck's nose touching the sign. They ordered the same as the last time. Gibson rested back in his chair and looked at the mirror behind the bar, thinking things over.

"Anatoe claimed he was getting a beer from Felton's house," Eckhart said.

"And nobody noticed him." Gibson took a taste of his burger.

"That's right, but David told us he thought Anatoe and Elsie were arguing by the landing. Although he wasn't a hundred percent positive, Mr. Tatlow was. Anatoe doesn't have an alibi. None that we have found yet. Why would he be quarreling with Elsie? Why go to the beach to start a fight with her? What would be so important?"

"That's a lot of questions," he said.

Eckhart wiped mustard off her mouth with a napkin and looked over at him. "Could it be that he just wanted to go out with her sister? That sounds so lame."

"We'll ask him again."

"He won't tell us."

"We'll see," Gibson said.

"Maybe the ring is his?"

"Could be."

"What about the Grimsby guys? Are they connected?"

"We'll check them out, too."

Eckhart plucked out her journal again and found the name she was looking for. "John Terry Henneberry. He's the president of that fraternity club. Should we phone ahead?"

"No, I think we'll make a surprise visit," Gibson replied, a small smile playing on his lips.

"Where has Gregory been? That's a problem. Don't you think? It's been a few days since anyone has seen him. Is he the killer and we're just letting him go?"

"I haven't forgotten about him. Maybe he went to Grimsby," he said.

"He should know that we would want to talk to him. After all, he found the body."

"We'll track him down. One way or the other."

"Okay. What about Mr. Tatlow?"

"He seemed harmless enough," Gibson said. "Or is he the monster the kids insist he is?" He didn't really think that was the case.

"Right. Who do you truly know?" Eckhart tempted him with her deep pools of blue. "You deserve a nightcap after listening to all that stuff about death on Lawsons Lane."

"I do." He knew what he was about to do was wrong, but he wanted this.

Eckhart chattered as she drove. Her laughter was like a songbird. He drank it all in, savouring the moment. She parked in the driveway and they scampered up the steps two at a time. A moon hung over the lake, spilling a silver light into the room. She held out her hand, and he took it. The kisses were long and deep. All thoughts of the future melted away in the heady lust. Afterward, he lay beside her and let himself dream of a different life.

Chapter 10

It had been a warm night with barely a breeze to cool his fevered body when Gibson stole his way out of the townhouse. He had taken one last glimpse before he closed the bedroom door, the moonlight shimmering on her smooth skin. Now he waited in the café for the Expedition to come round the corner. Eckhart smiled at him as he hopped into the truck.

"Hi, handsome." Her voice had a trace of huskiness that wasn't there yesterday.

Gibson felt at ease. She would always know what to say.

"It's time to see what the husband has to say," he said. Even to his own ears that sounded weird.

"I agree." She giggled like a school girl and glanced at him sideways, a faint curve of her mouth lingered.

Eckhart drove out of town and shortly after pulled into Jacobs Landing. She lined up the Expedition in front of the general store. Someone had ripped dead flowers from the terracotta urns and thrown them on the ground. They strolled under the covered passage—honeysuckle and purple-flowered clematis vines clinging to the lattice trellis—to the small forties bungalow at the back. It was isolated from the house next door by a tract of meadowland. He punched the buzzer. The peal reverberated inside. There was no other noise until the slapping of rubber echoed along the hallway. Savannah opened the door.

"May we come in?" Gibson asked.

"You're the detectives?"

He nodded.

They accompanied her down a short corridor, pictures covering the walls with their life. Gibson swept his eyes over the black and white and sepia photographs. Savannah led them to the kitchen, the sweet smell of coffee brewing. The room was bright and cheery, painted a bold yellow. Behind the glass-fronted cabinets was a mishmash of chinaware, doubtless collected since the fifties. A simple folded tea towel dangled from the oven handle. The rustic table took up most of the tiny space with old chairs crowded around. Probably antiques now.

Todd sat at the head of the table and nodded in their direction. He was dressed in the uniform of the grieving—sweat pants and a T-shirt. His hair was unruly, but he had shaven. A weighted look dragged his skin down in pale folds. Gibson hauled out a chair and sat down, glancing out the window to the fields beyond. Eckhart perched on a seat beside him. Savannah plunked down and brushed at her forehead.

"We're sorry for your loss."

"Thanks." Todd's lips were drawn in. A glassy look told them his spirit had retreated inward as well. Where else could he flee?

"Did you make it to the party?" Gibson asked.

"No, I was working on the books. I planned to make it before the fireworks started, but..."

"Someone heard Anatoe and Elsie arguing. Any idea what that would have been about?"

"I don't know. Maybe she told him to stay away from her sister."

Savannah dipped her chin at his remark and plucked her bangs.

"Would he have hurt Elsie?"

"No, not really." Todd sucked in his breath. "But I think Gregory would." His sidelong glance toward Savannah spoke volumes.

Savannah stared hard at him and then narrowed her eyes.

"What makes you say that?" Gibson asked.

"Because of his prior behavior," Todd said.

"What behaviour?" Gibson shook his head not following.

"He was in jail for raping a teenage girl." A haughty laugh escaped his lips.

Gibson shot a look toward Eckhart. Oh, shit. How did they miss that? Was it because he had other things on his mind?

Savannah sunk into her chair, sticking her fist to her mouth.

"His mother isn't much better either."

"Todd, stop that." Savannah lashed out. "Gregory didn't do anything. He didn't rape that girl. It was—"

Todd slammed his palm on the table. "He did two years for Christ sakes. What's the matter with you?" His voice cracked. The air was thick and heavy. A premonitory chill ran down Gibson's spine. The silence was like a shroud. It stretched thinner and thinner, ready to rupture.

"Did you see anything, Savannah?" Gibson pressed on.

"Like what?"

"Did you see anybody leave?"

"I guess Gregory left before the fireworks." She paused. "But so did a few of the other guys. So what."

"Anything else?"

Todd shrugged.

"No." Savannah looked up at him.

"Okay. Thanks for your help. Take care."

They trudged down the pathway to the truck. Gibson studied the shuttered windows of the store. "We have a dilemma."

"What?" Eckhart asked.

"Presumably Gregory is on parole."

"Oh."

"He may have breached his parole in several aspects."

"Such as?"

"Hanging out at a party with alcohol available. Alternatively, were there any adolescents present? We don't know his conditions of release."

"And he seems to be missing," Eckhart said.

"Yeah. Maybe that's why he's taken a runner. Let's go to the station."

"Maybe catch a snack on the way."

"Sure," he replied.

She fired up the Expedition. They stopped at a local takeout and snagged sandwiches and coffee. He ate his veggie roll on the road. There wasn't a soul in the office. The constables had taken off for the day.

They headed to Eckhart's office. It was painted a light shade of yellow with cream coloured baseboards. Limited edition prints hung on one wall. A naked oak desk faced the door, a power position for the boss. The floor-to-ceiling window behind it overlooked the same row of maples as the other offices. A bookshelf bursting with law books took up the rest of the room.

"Nice."

"I'm partial to it." Eckhart pulled a laptop out of a top drawer and placed it on the desk. It fired up but there wasn't any internet access. "My computer isn't hooked up yet."

"Oh."

They headed to the lab, brushing hands as they squeezed through the doorway.

"Nothing yet," Frenchy said before they asked.

"Can we use the computer?"

"You bet." She punched in her password. "There you go."

Gibson sat down and logged into the RCMP database. He scrolled through a few pages before he found Gregory Cunningham.

"Yup. He's on parole." He looked up at his partner.

"What are the conditions?"

"The regular. He can't leave the city. He must keep the peace. Be of good behaviour and obey the law. Duh."

Eckhart giggled.

"Abstain from alcohol and illegal drugs. Forbidden to contact victims or children. Stay away from people involved in criminal activity. Not allowed to keep any weapon. That's it."

"Has he broken any of the conditions?"

"If he consumed beer with the guys," he answered.

"Okay."

"One further condition I see here." He passed his finger down the screen. "If you have been arrested or questioned by the police, you must notify your supervisor immediately. That doesn't help. We can't question someone we can't find. So, has Gregory made himself scarce because he's afraid of being involved – because of his parole? Or the worst-case scenario we have to consider is, did he kill Elsie?"

"Oh, god," Eckhart said.

"His parole can be suspended for up to fourteen days even if there's a suspicion he has violated his release conditions."

"I would hide from us too." Another giggle erupted.

"He can be arrested and returned to jail."

"We better talk to his parole officer."

"Maybe there's a number online." He searched through the webpage. "Nope."

"Call the central switchboard."

"You should do that. You have the right badge." Gibson chuckled.

She stabbed in the numbers and waited. "Hi, there. This is Inspector Rene Eckhart. I'm looking for a contact number for a parole officer." She rattled off her badge number and Gregory's full name and address. An elevator song trumpeted into the earpiece. She yanked the phone from her ear and pouted. The operator returned within a few minutes and provided her the info. Eckhart hung up and shifted to Gibson.

"Brandon Sullivan." She dialed, but the call flipped to an agent. Brandon was out of town, so she made an appointment for when he returned.

"We have an appointment for Sunday at ten."

"We need to find Gregory. Where would he have gone?"

"I think you might be right. He's gone to Grimsby."

"If we find him there, that would be an infringement of his parole," Gibson said. "We'll go tomorrow."

"Right. Early morning then?"

"Pick me up at seven?"

"Okay." She bit her tongue.

They cruised down the service road to the main street and through Port Dalhousie. She pulled into the motel's circular driveway and shifted into park. She watched him go in the front entrance and drove home.

Chapter 11

The grim twist of Gibson's mouth revealed his sombre mood. He stood outside the café waiting for his ride, leaning against the building, hands in his pockets. Not even the sun-kissed sky caused him to smile. He watched as thin, feathery clouds drifted lazily through the forget-me-not blue.

Eckhart pulled up in the truck. What attracted him to her beauty, her silliness? The doubts had started to creep in. The last few years had been challenging. Was he burned out? Or looking for a way out? He wasn't certain. Yes, he loved Katherine, but something had become buried in the struggles. He slid into the passenger seat.

"Hi, cowboy. It's been a few rough days." She tapped lightly on his sleeve and lifted her eyebrows mischievously.

Gibson flashed a quirky smile and stretched out for the run to Grimsby, gazing out the window. She turned around in the motel parking lot and took Ontario Street to the Queen Elizabeth Highway West, four lanes in each direction. Large trucks shook the Expedition as they rocketed past. Gibson sank deeper into his seat and tried to enjoy the ride. The road ran parallel to the shoreline with scenery that replayed itself every so often: trees, fields, houses; repeat.

When they reached Jordan Harbour, the highway converged with the lake. Gibson looked at the never-ending expanse of light-dappled water. Just as he had focused on the horizon, Eckhart swung the truck inland. Ten minutes later, Gibson spotted the turnoff for Beamsville.

"There's our exit. I haven't been out this way for thirty years."

"Really?"

Eckhart took the off ramp and circled round the overpass. She zigzagged through the back roads. They passed several vineyards, acres of greenhouses and apple orchards before Lincoln Avenue came up at a crossroads.

Gibson considered the signpost. The numbering was faded. Which way to go? "Turn right." Just before some railroad tracks, he saw a mailbox on the roadside with the address they were searching. He pointed to the run-down house. "Here."

It was more like a shack, black stains running down the siding, moss on the roof.

Eckhart pulled behind an old Ford Escort with rusted-out fenders. Two kids came shooting around the corner, torn shorts and dirt covered knees. They stopped and gawked at the gleaming new truck. She shut off the motor. "What's this guy's name again?"

"JT Henneberry," he said, reading from his notes.

They stepped out into a drier, warmer air than the city, away from the water. A skinny boy ran straight at Gibson, head down like a battering ram.

"Whoa there, big fellow." He chuckled.

"Are you a friend of my dad?" the boy asked, swaggering on a pinpoint, fixed to rumble.

"Ah. Could be."

The front door lurched open. A skinny guy stood there with a cigarette dangling from his mouth. He wore jeans tattered at the hem and a T-shirt with a label from some rock band.

"You must be the detectives."

Anatoe had given JT a heads up.

"Come on in." They strode along a well-rutted track across a brown yard, the two kids shoving in behind. "You guys go play."

"I want to see too," the boy whined in a squeaky, high-pitched cry.

"I don't think so. Beat it."

Both children raced to the rear, shrieking and howling with delight.

"Kids."

The interior wasn't much better than the exterior. Patches of mold mottled the dirt-encrusted windows. The walls had turned from an off-white to an off-yellow from tobacco. The living room had three couches, each rattier than the next. They were wedged into an unbelievably tiny space. A coffee table held several ashtrays, not overflowing, but getting there. Eckhart scrunched her face, wiggling her snout. The place smelled bad, smoky and of dead stuff.

"Have a seat." JT punched out a puff of blue smoke toward the ceiling.

Both detectives made their way through the toy trap and squatted on the brink of their chairs. Eckhart squirmed. JT plunged backward into his spot—front line to the television, remote on the arm of the lounge.

"So, what's up?" A red stone on his hand flashed even in the dingy light.

Gibson recognized the ring.

"You were at the fireworks? At Felton's house, right?" he asked.

"Yup."

"Who did you come down with?"

"Logan, my buddy. He drove. Let me think. Joe and Ben." He crushed his fag into the closest ashtray. A quantity of butts slipped onto the table.

"Last names?"

Eckhart scribbled in her journal, puckering her lips, trying not to inhale.

"Are they all from the same fraternity?" Gibson asked.

"Yeah, sure. Alpha Zee." JT peered at Eckhart and presented a lopsided smirk. He crossed his tongue over his bottom lip. She ignored him.

"We found this at the crime scene." Gibson plucked a photo from his pocket and tossed it over.

"Not mine," JT said and flashed his ring in front of his face.

"I see that. Anybody missing one?"

"Not sure." He picked up his pack of smokes, studied Eckhart, and then pitched them back onto the coffee table.

"Any guesses?" Gibson asked.

"How should I know? Maybe an ex-girlfriend or something?"

"Have you seen Gregory lately?" Gibson thrust that in as indifferently as he could.

"No. Not since the fireworks."

"How did you happen to even be there?"

"Blinkers invited us," JT said.

"Who?"

"Anatoe. We call him Blinkers. You know. His eye." JT smirked.

"Why did he invite you? Because you're fraternity brothers."

"No. He's a cousin of sorts. He shows up here all the time. Usually on weekends."

"When was he out last?"

"A month ago, I guess?" JT replied.

"Okay. So back to the fireworks. Did any of you guys leave before they started?"

"No. What do you mean?"

"Go down to the beach?" Gibson asked.

"No." JT narrowed his eyes. "None of us even knew Elsie if that's what you're getting at?" He hesitated. "I've met Todd though."

"What? Her husband?"

"Yeah, he was here one day, hunting down Anatoe."

Gibson took a quick look at Eckhart and glowered. "When was this?"

"A month ago. He paraded in, right after Anatoe got here."

Eckhart watched him light up another fag. JT trapped the smoke in his mouth. He blew swirls out between his lips into perfect rings that scattered when they hit the wall. She felt dizzy and coughed, trying hard not to let it turn into a long fit of choking. Gibson remained mum, letting the guy reveal the story his own way. When JT flicked the cigarette toward the ashtray, the ash sprinkled onto the rug. He inhaled another round and continued.

"Todd confronted Anatoe. Told him to stay away from Savannah. Anatoe was chill though. Offered him a beer and they talked. Todd stuck around for several hours." He crushed the butt and stared at Gibson with hardened eyes and a clenched jaw.

Gibson gestured, giving permission to proceed.

"Some ladies came over. It turned into a party. Todd became chummy with Sue. I think it was her. I was tipsy by then. He took off with someone."

A ghost walked through Gibson. He shivered. "Are you claiming he left with a young woman?"

"Yeah, that's precisely what I'm saying."

"Oh, shit." Gibson muttered under his breath.

Eckhart placed her hand over her mouth.

"So, you have a number or address?"

"No, I don't know her personally, but Cindy will," JT said.

Eckhart wrote in her notebook.

Gibson stood up. He turned toward the door. When he got there, he looked back at JT. "Don't call her," he said stiffly.

The guy lit up another smoke and shrugged. The kids came flying at the sound of the Expedition firing up. They pawed at the clean truck, leaving baby prints along the bottom panels.

"Take us for a spin?"

Eckhart rolled down the window. "Not today. Look out. Don't want to run you over."

The boy snatched his younger brother's hand and tugged him aside. Eckhart backed up warily and tooted the horn as they rode away.

"Holy shit! Todd. Did he cheat on Elsie?" Eckhart said.

"Let's find out. Cindy's place is just off Kerman Road. Not far from here."

After a few turns in the road, they made it to their destination. Gibson pointed to a modest dwelling adjacent to the freeway, massive power lines passing through the neighbourhood. "Bet you can hear those suckers buzz in the rain."

"Yuck."

"JT said on the right side. Basement suite."

"Okay."

Gibson rapped lightly on the doorframe. No answer, so he knocked again. A crack opened. A young girl with snarled hair and shabby clothes peered through the slim gap. She was scrawny as if drugs had a grip on her.

"What do you want?"

"Are you Cindy?"

"Who wants to know?" She eyed them suspiciously.

Oh brother. Gibson pulled out his badge.

"Yeah." She shrunk into herself.

"Do you know Sue Reynolds?"

"Yeah."

"Do you have a number for her?"

"No." She pushed on the door to close it.

"JT says you do." Gibson stuck his foot in the way.

"My cell isn't working."

"Address?" Gibson barked.

She gave them an address and shut out the world with a bang.

* * *

The ancient wood-framed apartment on Parker Road was easy to locate because he knew someone that had lived nearby from that long-ago time. The rumble of a thousand automobiles resonated down the street from the highway barely a spit's distance to the north. They slipped through the unsecured entrance and walked down a corridor that stank of a concoction of several countries. Gibson knocked on the flimsy door. A woman responded instantly. She lifted her eyebrows at his handsome face, flipped her mane and suggested in a silky voice, "May I help you?" She batted her lashes. Suddenly, she detected Eckhart standing at the side. She pouted, drawing her red lips down at the corners.

"Are you Sue Reynolds?" Gibson flashed his badge.

"Yes." She reached back and gathered her locks into a bunch, twisting a scrunchy off her wrist to secure her hair into a high ponytail. "Oh, come on in."

They went down a tight hallway to a respectable living room, painted a pastel colour. The sliding door faced the freeway. The detectives sat on a pink lounge covered with a quilt made up of every shade of pink imaginable. Sue perched herself on the edge of a loveseat.

"Do you know a Todd Webber?"

"I don't think so." She batted her lashes.

"He was at JT's place. A friend of Anatoe—"

"Oh, yeah. I remember him. He was kinda cute." She flung him a perky smile.

"Did he come home with you?"

"No. That wasn't me. Who told you that?"

"JT."

"He's wrong. That guy left with JoJo."

Gibson gave her a look.

"Josephine Black."

"Are you certain?" Gibson grumbled.

"Yeah, I'm sure. I had to drive them. They were extremely drunk." She paused. "We have the same colour hair. You know. Guess that's why JT figured it was me." She flicked her ponytail.

"Got a number and address?"

"Yeah, sure." She rolled through her cell contacts. "Here it is."

"Thanks."

Eckhart jotted in her journal.

They walked through the international corridor and headed back to the truck. Gibson glimpsed at the sky. The sun was already pushing west. He jumped into the Expedition and slammed the door. Eckhart stared at him curiously.

"Sorry. I guess I'm getting hungry." He blew out a huge breath. "This better be the very last one."

"No kidding."

He grew quiet, his eyes focused on a mark on the carpeting. Eckhart turned toward him, but said nothing. She drove to Slessor Boulevard. It was a newer high-rise building. In the lobby they scanned the directory. Gibson pressed the intercom.

"Hello." A pleasant voice answered.

"Hi, Josephine Black? It's the police. May we come in and speak to you?"

"What's it about?"

"Todd Webber?"

"Oh."

The line made a buzzing sound, and then the door squawked. He grabbed at the handle. They entered a decent hallway and took an elevator to the seventh floor. A woman who looked similar to Sue stood in a doorway half way down. Her hair was braided into two plaits, hanging on either side of her oval face. She wore Bermuda shorts and a short-sleeved blouse. They were led into a living room with plush furniture and a great view of the water to the north. He looked across the lake to the skyscrapers of Toronto silhouetted against the sapphire sky. A cat strolled into the room and wove itself between Eckhart's calves. He purred softly, and then leaped onto a platform near the window. There was a slight smell of kitty litter wafting in from the kitchen.

"Have a seat." Josephine sank onto the couch.

Eckhart plunked in an armchair beside a thin, sleek TV screen mounted above the fireplace. Gibson sat with his back to the vista.

"Are you having an affair with Todd?" he asked.

"Ah. Sort of."

"Sort of?"

"We met at a party a few weeks ago. At JT's. We hit it off right away, and he stayed the night. I realize he's married, but he said he would call."

"You mean leave his wife," Gibson snorted.

"Yeah, I suppose." Josephine looked down, unable to face his steel-grey eyes.

"Did he?"

"Did he what?"

"Call you?"

"No."

"Did you phone him?" Gibson raised his voice.

"Once."

"Once?" he said, sounding unconvinced.

"Three times." She hoisted her chin.

"What happened?"

"He said to stop calling him."

Gibson stood up unexpectedly. The rapid movement alarmed the cat. The animal bolted out of the room, nails scratching the floors trying to get a purchase on the polished wood.

"Someone murdered Todd's wife. I suggest you don't call again," he snapped, a sharp edge to his warning.

"Oh, my god." She gulped a mouthful of air.

Eckhart stiffened in her chair. Gibson rolled his eyes toward the door. They took off without ceremony, riding the elevator without speaking. He wasn't positive whom he was more furious with. Todd or Josephine? However, Todd had some explaining to do. Could he have murdered his wife?

"Lunch?" Eckhart asked, cutting off Gibson's reflections.

"Yeah."

She parked on Centre Street beneath a massive steel banner that spanned the road. It announced they were in 'Downtown Grimsby'. The Number Five Pub was a rustic tavern with a cozy atmosphere. They sat by a large window with swags for curtains. The tables were spaced close together to accommodate the weekend crowds, although it was a little slow right now. The bar took up a full wall, with the expected mirror behind. Toward the back, there were several booths with red cushioned seats. A family of four with rambunctious kids scooting under the table and generally fooling around, was a little distracting. In the next booth, a pretty brunette nearing the fifty mark was sitting alone. Her hand fingered the book on the table with deftness. He wouldn't have recognized her except for the soulful brown eyes that radiated warmth and made you feel at home.

He had his answer and dropped his gaze.

Eckhart turned to look at the lady in the booth. Her eyes flashed a spark of green.

"Do you know her?"

"No." But he did.

They ate their meal in silence, the first sign of awkwardness between them.

"Are you ready?" Eckhart asked.

"Yeah, let's get going."

She cruised down the freeway in the fast lane. Gibson leaned into the bucket seat, glancing at the speedometer with the corner of his eye—the Expedition sneered at the speed limit. He watched the scenery blur past his vision, the pattern of traffic lights mesmerizing. The truck snaked down the side roads and climbed the curb at his motel.

"Pick you up at nine?"

"You bet." Gibson slipped off the soft leather and into the warm night. Fireflies flicked off and on as they darted through the air. The black and white checkerboard tile in the lobby seemed out of place today. He trod wearily down the corridor to his room and collapsed onto the bed. His unmoving gaze looked inward. Should he call Katherine? It was invariably a crapshoot guessing what mood she would be in. That was part of the problem. He shut his eyes and released his breath. He sensed the stress drain from his body as he drifted into the limbo of dreams.

Chapter 12

Gibson was at the coffee shop at eight. The blues twisted his heart, plagued by the past and troubled by the future. He sipped his drink with intent, thinking of an adage he had heard long ago. 'If you don't know what to do. Do nothing'. Something like that. Kind of made sense. The status quo was safer than stepping off the cliff. Then Eckhart moved into his field of view, the light dancing on her bronzed skin. He moaned and grazed his forehead with his fingertips.

Eckhart appeared relaxed when he hopped into the truck. She turned and faced his way. There was laughter on her mind. A sweet smile with just a hint of shyness curved her lips.

"What?" Gibson asked.

"I have a sense about today."

"About Gregory?"

"Yes. It's Sunday. I think he'll show up at home. Should we—"

"Stick to the plan. See what Brandon has to disclose," Gibson interrupted. At this point, he realized she was very keen to pin this on Gregory before the facts.

"You're right. Our appointment first."

They cruised downtown to Church Street. Vehicles were plodding slowly down the road, lots of hesitation and testing out possible parking spots. Some trying to manoeuvre into a tiny space, others vacillating and moving on. Six churches within two blocks on a Sunday morning.

"There's a parking lot at the back of the station," she said.

She pulled around the corner. A substantial metal barrier closed the entrance. "Oh, shit." She drove another block before encountering a space.

They strolled down the sidewalk enjoying the cooler day. Gibson scrutinized the distinctive architectural styles of the buildings. A dedicated flock emptied from a creamy white church, streaming down massive stone steps in groups of three and four. The copper spires on its roof gleamed in the sunlight. He stopped to admire rose-coloured gargoyles on lofty perches on an ancient brick structure set back from the road. It was almost ten by the time they arrived at the parole service.

The Government of Canada Building was a two-storey edifice of Federal Heritage designation near City Hall. Its exterior veneer of yellow limestone and black granite was intriguing. The central entrance had an arched facade with a metal Canadian coat of arms mounted on the wall: *A Mari Usque Ad Mare*—From Sea to Sea.

Gibson seized the magnificent brass handle and hauled on the weighty glass door. They entered a vast main vestibule, light ricocheting off the white, polished marble surfaces. Eckhart's shoes clicked on the terrazzo tile. As they walked up the granite steps, he passed his palm along the sleek chrome railing. A broad arrow pointed them in the appropriate direction. They advanced the length of a wide corridor to room 206. An older black man hunched over a tiny pressed wood desk appeared busy with his elbows leaned on top and jaw in hand. He looked attentively at the pages as he flipped through the folder. At the sharp rap on the doorframe, he raised his head. Brown eyes sparkled in a wizened face. A genuine smile made him look approachable. He vaulted out of his chair and moved round to receive the detectives.

"I'm always glad to meet up with the police." An upper-class voice rang out. His grip was cool and firm. A self-assured man who had been around the block more than once. He maintained a well-timed eye lock with Gibson, and threw him a modest nod.

"Have a seat." He gestured to the chairs in front of his desk. "Just leafing through Gregory's file. The clerk informed me you have issues with my newest parolee."

"More a worry," Gibson replied.

"He was an ideal inmate at the detention centre. I like the guy. Tell me what's going on."

"We're investigating a homicide on Lawsons Lane."

"Okay. That's the street I have for Gregory," Brandon said, tracing his finger along the sheet.

"The incident took place on the beach adjacent to the Cunningham home. Felton and Margaret's house."

"I understand." He furrowed his eyebrows. "So how does that connect to my guy exactly?"

"Do you have a specific interest in Gregory?" Gibson studied the officer. He needed to learn how much Brandon would defend.

"Yes. I always read my clients' files. His case seems flimsy on details. I would hate to see it happen again."

"We have nothing definitive at this time. But Gregory discovered the body." Gibson paused when he noticed Brandon incline his head. "Which doesn't mean a thing, but he ran off and hasn't been seen since. That was a week ago."

"That's a headache for you."

"We figured he may have breached his conditions of discharge. Well, not all. But..."

"What condition?" Brandon asked.

"The crime took place during a fireworks gathering at his dad's house."

"Oh. Alcohol, drugs and maybe teenagers."

"I haven't confirmed he was drinking or doing drugs. It was an adult party; no kids were there."

"So, the real problem is he's missing," Brandon said.

"Yes. I suppose that's it in a nutshell." Gibson frowned at his lack of direction.

"If Gregory has left the district, I can have him picked up. But you don't know that for a fact if you can't find him." He grinned and looked back at his journal. "I'm not expecting to see him until..." Brandon flipped forward two pages, "Tuesday."

"He might show up at home today. It's Sunday dinner day," Eckhart said.

"I have no reason to issue a warrant. But we have a legal right to go through his living quarters without cause. I could offer you approval for that."

"That would be excellent," Gibson said. "But if we turn up anything that ties him to our case, we'll have to apprehend him."

Brandon leaned back into his chair and set his palms behind his head, staring at the ceiling and said, "Do me a favour. Call me if that happens. I won't retract his parole unless it is something incriminating. He gets a fourteen-day grace. Let's see what you discover first."

"Fair enough." Gibson reached over the desk and shook his hand. "We'll be in contact."

The detectives scampered down the steps, reverberations of their footfalls bouncing off the marble as they launched out the exit. Eckhart's eyes were alight with expectation. She wanted to waltz down the pavement.

"This is it."

"Don't get ahead of yourself." Gibson suspected he was marching into a tempest. His eyebrows were compressed together in trepidation.

"It's Gregory. I know it. Don't be absurd." Eckhart jabbed his shoulder and sprinted to the truck.

Gibson raced behind her. Eckhart fired up the motor and ripped away from the curb before he had his seatbelt fastened. He seized the dashboard and held on for the ride. There wasn't much traffic, so she tore down the street. Before she could flip a switch on the panel, he gave her a look.

"We don't need the siren and lights."

"Okay. If you say so." Her mouth lifted upward, crinkling her dimples. The smile reached her eyes, the deep pools of blue. She giggled.

Gibson pushed into the leather and closed his eyes. The growl of the tires on a metal grate alerted him to his whereabouts. He glanced to the side to catch the stern of the biggest ship he had seen so far. It sunk low. The wash left behind mushroomed out in a vast fan, striking the canal sides, and boomed back. The water bubbled in every direction.

Eckhart turned down Lawsons Lane and deliberately inched down the roadway. She pulled into the entrance and shut off the engine. Her hands fluttered on the steering wheel. She drew in a sharp gasp.

"Gregory's here. I'm ready."

Gibson looked past the motorbike parked next to Felton's vehicle to a figure in the dahlia bed. Margaret glanced up and bestowed a wave, secateurs in her grip. The straw hat perched on her frizzy hair was secured with a bow under her double chin. Someone had propped a bucket packed with dead flowers against a dirt pile. A slight grin screwed her lip. She ambled toward them, her clogs slapping on her feet.

"What brings you out here?"

"To see Gregory," Eckhart said.

"They're inside." Margaret trudged up the stairs, the two detectives right behind. She yanked off her hat and tossed it on the ottoman. Muffled voices and a wisp of smoke slipped through the screen. Margaret snatched the handle and swung the door open forcefully.

"What did I tell you about smoking in the house?"

"My leg aches."

"Put it out," she growled.

"There. Happy now?" Felton ground his cigarette in an ashtray and scowled.

Margaret seized a tea towel and flung it around in the air, driving smoke out the door. Felton rubbed his thighs, muttering. "Can't do what I want in my own house."

Gibson held back a smirk.

Gregory remained frozen in his chair. His posture was rigid, his expression dull as he gazed at the worn linoleum. His breathing was virtually undetectable.

"We've been looking everywhere for you." Eckhart stood over him, fists on her hips.

"I didn't do anything." Gregory squirmed, eyes everywhere except on the detective.

Gibson pointed his chin at Eckhart indicating for her to take a seat. Felton plucked out his filthy handkerchief and coughed up phlegm. Margaret plopped herself down, arranging her secateurs on the table. The inspector sat next to Gregory, swung toward him and leaned in.

"Where have you been?" Gibson asked.

"At a friend's house."

"In town?"

"Yeah." The lie slipped out, smooth and easy like an orange cello shot.

"You found Elsie on the beach," Gibson said.

Gregory blinked.

"Did you see what happened?"

"No." He shifted in his seat.

"Was she dead when you found her?"

"Yeah." He wavered. "I..."

Margaret bristled. Gibson held up a hand.

"Did you touch her?"

"No."

"Okay. What did you do after that?"

"I ran up the stairs. Jackie was there. I told her Elsie was dead. Then I got the hell out of there." He paused. "I don't know why. Jackie yelled, but I couldn't go back."

"Why is that Gregory?"

"Because I knew you would blame me." His voice went shrill.

Margaret worked her mouth, gnawing on the inside of her cheek. Gibson shot her a warning.

"Because you're on parole?"

Gregory formed fists, his lips clamped together.

Gibson plucked the photograph out of his upper pocket and passed it to Gregory. "Is this your ring?"

A weak squeak from across the table.

"I don't think so." He flinched, jerking backward. Two crimson spots grew on his cheeks, a sharp contrast to his chalk-white complexion.

"You're not wearing one."

"I put it aside when I…" A thickness in his throat stopped him.

"Should we go find it?" Gibson asked.

"Are you allowed to look at my stuff?" His eyes popped with panic.

"Yes, as part of your release conditions—"

The detective didn't finish the sentence before Gregory propelled his chair from the table and jumped up. His face was pale and blank. His motions perfunctory. The detectives accompanied him down the corridor. Gibson expected clothes to be scattered about and a locker-room funk to linger in the air. Instead, the quilt on the bed lay smoothed, folded down from the pillow. In a corner, a guitar was cradled in a stand. Nothing was pitched on the floor.

"It should be here somewhere. I can't remember." Gregory rummaged through the drawers of a Tallboy dresser. He shrugged his shoulders and gave a slow shake of his head.

"Could it be in here?" Gibson asked as he opened the closet door. A whiff of copper escaped. He glanced over to alert Eckhart that something was up. Gregory's body slumped. Margaret forced herself forward, aggression building on her mouth. Eckhart barred the entrance and stood fast against the elbow jabbed into her rib cage.

"What's going on?" Margaret asked.

Gibson snapped on gloves. He poked through a laundry basket and plucked up a shirt concealed at the bottom. It was discolored with a sticky substance. He dropped it back.

"Eckhart."

"We're taking you in for questioning." She sailed across the room in one large stride, cuffs at the ready, twirled Gregory around and clamped on the restraints.

"What the hell!" Margaret shouted.

"Margaret, go sit down." The explosive bark stunned everyone into silence. It was the first manifestation of Gibson's pit-bull demeanour since his arrival east.

"Gregory you have violated your conditions of release—"

"No. I was trying to help Elsie."

"Shut up, Gregory," Margaret snarled. She hovered in the background. Her clodhoppers clunking as she paced in front of the doorway.

"As I was saying, a suspicion of being implicated in a crime is all I need to hold you. Your parole isn't revoked yet, and you aren't under arrest. However, you'll be in lockup downtown until further notice. Do you understand?"

"Yes," Gregory answered. He swallowed hard, sucking his lips inward.

Gibson drew out his cell and called Frenchy. "We're at Felton and Margaret's place. We discovered some bloodied clothes. Could you get here ASAP?"

"On my way." She hung up.

"I'll alert Brandon," Gibson said and perched on the bed to wait for the forensics.

Eckhart steered Gregory past his mom.

"You can't do this," Margaret hissed, spit flying from her twisted mouth as they pushed out the door.

Gregory remained on the rear bench of the Expedition, slumped so low he sank from sight. Frenchy tore into the driveway forty-five minutes later. Eckhart leaned against the hood of her vehicle and signaled to the house. With a case fastened to her side, Frenchy vaulted up the steps. She gave a quick rap on the door and strode right in.

Felton blew smoke rings across the room. Margaret sat fixed, a scowl tracing lines along her face. Frenchy cracked a modest grin and called out down the hallway.

"Gibson?"

"I'm back here."

She followed the sound. "Tidy."

"Yeah."

"You seem kinda put out. What's up?" she asked.

He shrugged with one shoulder and pointed to the closet. "In there."

"You bet."

"Catch you later."

Margaret shrieked at them as Eckhart backed out of the driveway. Felton hobbled to the porch and lit another cigarette. Gibson was worried. What motive did Gregory have to kill Elsie? Nothing came to mind. His partner sure thought he was guilty. She drummed her fingers on the steering wheel. In the back, Gregory had retreated into a blackness he knew well.

* * *

The RCMP depot was next to the Parole Board at the rear of City Hall. All the church-goers had fled home for lunch, leaving bunches of parking spots. However, Eckhart had phoned ahead and the steel barrier to the lot was unlocked. Over the door, the stone lintel was engraved

'Police Headquarters'. They marched into the station unfettered.

A big old clock hung on the wall behind the desk sergeant at the front reception. The second hand swept smoothly around and around, ticking away the lives of the people in the building. The sergeant greeted them with a gruff smile. A leather-bound book lay on the counter in front of him. He recorded their arrival taking note of the person in custody and the detectives' badge numbers. He wrote with a flourish, proud to be doing things the old-fashioned way still.

The large room was an open-plan space with two rows of battered oak desks facing each other. A few of them were currently occupied by uniforms that were busy typing or on phones. The sergeant motioned for an officer to take Gregory into custody. With hands still cuffed, he dragged his feet down the long hallway, not glancing back even once. Eckhart chatted up the sergeant, leaning into the counter with her hip. Gibson rested on the bench against the wall and dialed the superintendent. Despite Rodney's office being located upstairs, it was Sunday, so he would be somewhere else having fun. After giving Rodney an update, Gibson hung up the phone. He struggled to get comfortable on the hard, wooden surface.

"Inspector."

Gibson looked up.

"Hi, Brandon."

"I take it you uncovered something."

Gibson gave the parole officer the details.

"It's sketchy. Gregory could have gotten blood on himself by leaning over Elsie to check her pulse, to see if she was still alive."

Gibson nodded in agreement.

"No. He did it. Gregory has a propensity for violence. And he fled the scene of a crime like a guilty person," Eckhart said, her voice rising with each accusation.

Nevertheless, Gibson recognized that more evidence would be needed—his fingerprint on the rock would do.

"And the ring," Eckhart added.

"Can I speak to him?" Brandon asked.

"Yeah. Tell him to get a lawyer," Gibson said.

"Thanks. I'll keep in touch."

They shook hands. Brandon strode down to the holding area with a police officer. The detectives left. Nothing more for them to do here.

Eckhart danced down the sidewalk, humming a secret tune. Gibson walked casually along, too many conflicting notions on his mind. He stubbed his toe on an irregular section of concrete. "Shit, that hurts."

Her sweet, joyful laughter echoed off the niches and gables in the glut of churches.

"Late lunch?"

"Sure," Gibson replied.

They walked down the street to the Mansion.

"I feel positive. My first case solved. How about some free time for tomorrow? We have to wait for the processing anyway," Eckhart said. Her lips puckered, hinting at something more.

"I agree. I have something to do." His eyes brightened. A spin in a kayak sounded promising. He wasn't as sure about Gregory though, but he pushed that thought aside for another day.

Chapter 13

"It's all your fault," Margaret howled. The sound warped down the line like a boom of thunder.

"What the hell are you talking about?" Savannah screeched back.

"They're your friends."

"Who?"

"David and Jackie."

"So?"

"So, they said it was Gregory who killed Elsie. Now he's been arrested." Margaret slammed down the phone.

Savannah moaned and slithered down the wall, rubbing at her face, tears forming. Whom could she call? She wiped the moisture from her cheeks.

Todd's footfalls made no sound at all. He stood over her crumpled form.

"What the hell?" Her watery eyes widened.

"What's the matter?"

"You scared me."

"What are you doing on the floor?"

"Gregory's been arrested."

"Oh, my god." Todd sniffed deeply, an edge of his lip trembling. He collapsed into the nearest armchair. "Why would he...?"

"It can't be true." Tears welled up anew. "I don't believe it."

"He was there." His voice became icy.

"Todd." Her chin thrust high, an unblinking gaze resting on his face. He couldn't make eye contact.

"I'm sorry. I realize you like Gregory." He put folded hands on the table. "But if..."

"Let's leave it for now." Savannah stood up and set the kettle on for tea.

* * *

Gibson took an Uber to Henley Island. He had been a spectator at the Royal Henley Regatta long ago, but now he wanted to test the waters for himself. He wandered over to the clubhouse. Racks of rowing shells hung off the outer wall. He glanced through the wide shop door. The crews had packed rows of shelves with oars, floating devises and jackets to the roof peak. A few people milled around looking busy.

"Can I help you?" An energized lad darted over.

"Sure. Where are the kayak rentals?"

"Just follow the path. There's a shack by the dock." He pointed to the left.

Gibson skipped diagonally over a grassy field shaded by huge trees. Visitors were picnicking on rough wooden benches, the kids playing tag. Two teenagers were attempting to fly a kite with no wind. He followed the track down stone steps to the water.

Martindale Pond shimmered in the sunlight. Several teams were skimming across the pond in eight-man boats, practicing for the upcoming events. Luckily for boaters, the reservoir created during the development of the original Welland Canal had been abandoned for their enjoyment.

Gibson set himself up with a kayak and shoved off to explore. He dipped the paddles from side to side and traveled east. Following the shoreline, he observed interesting canal ruins and a dam. He swung the boat west to Richardson Creek and stayed for a snack, leaning against the backrest, letting his face catch the full beam of the sun. From there, he paddled to the south toward Twelve Mile Creek. It was more dangerous in this section with currents churning up the water. After five hours, he was confident he had discovered the entire area and headed back to the old dock.

Gibson stopped in Port Dalhousie at Harry's Diner. Fish and chips, a beer and a view of Lake Ontario was a good way to end a perfect day. After dinner, a friendly Uber driver took him to his motel. It was getting late, and suddenly he wondered what Katherine was up to. Why hadn't she phoned? He picked up his cell and stabbed at the speed dial for home.

"Hello." She was panting.

"Are you okay?"

"I had to rush for the phone."

"What's going on?"

"Oh, didn't I tell you? Heather had a showing at a gallery in Vancouver."

"Honestly? Good for her. She makes beautiful watercolours," Gibson said. "Did you go?"

"Yeah, we stayed downtown. I had a manicure and pedicure. Naturally, after that, I roamed the stores for new shoes." She laughed. "A lady knows what she likes. Right?"

"That's great. We have some progress here, but I'll be a few days further." Gibson thought to himself, don't make it a whopping lie. "Maybe a week." He sucked in his breath and waited.

"No big deal. I miss you, but I have more interviews. So I'm pretty busy. Love you."

A life-size smooch zoomed down the phone line. Gibson laid his head on the pillow and drifted off, his soul torn.

* * *

Eckhart headed toward town, shifted south to Glendale Avenue and out toward the countryside. After she passed the sanatorium, the road swayed with the contours of the valley. Within a half an hour, Dead Man's Curve made itself known. It was a perilous part of the original freeway. The switchback swerved sharply to the left before its precipitous decline, forcing a diligent driver to slow down. Those that didn't pay heed flirted with danger. She geared down to execute the ridge. From the bottom, it was clear sailing to the sleepy township of Fonthill. The crossroads had a gas station, general store, greasy spoon restaurant and a deli; all with jam-packed parking lots. She went east. A couple more bends and she drew into an extensive paved entrance. The residence rose a hundred metres from the road isolated by a fringe of maples. The two-storey yellow brick building had several chimneys poking out of a blue metal roof. A broad wooden porch wrapped around to the side with a double set of steps leading to a cabana. The door lurched open before she exited the truck.

"Hi, Mom. I thought I would stop for a short visit. How are you doing?" Eckhart asked.

"Fine, dear. Come sit down."

Eckhart followed her mother through a foyer with a high ceiling, a chandelier hanging in the vast opening, to the family room that looked out onto the infinity pool. A breeze pushed tiny waves across the crystal water. Spray from the waterfall attracted a pair of sparrows. They flapped their wings in the fountain, and then bolted into the bushes.

"What are you up to?"

"I just made my first collar as inspector. So I got the day off. Isn't that great?"

"Tell me more about that inspector from Vancouver."

"Victoria, Mom. Yeah, he's real nice," Eckhart replied. She opened and closed her mouth as if she had more to say.

"But?"

"He's married." She paused and added, "but I don't think he's happy."

"Well, be careful. You know what happened last time," her mom said.

"Yeah. I gotta go." She glanced at her watch.

Eckhart headed to the front door, her mom trailing behind. Why did she bother coming here with her problems? She should have known better. Maybe Mom was right. Leave the man alone. She hopped into the truck and sped out the sweeping drive to her private club—Royal St. Kitts. She had been a member since she was twelve. As a junior, she had free-range access, weekly lessons and cheap golf. In return, she had picked up stray balls for the pro shop. The hackers hit everywhere—in the ditches, over the net and down the road. A few landed on the roof overhang. Now, she was a full-fledged associate and could easily lose herself on the course. The feel of the manicured fairway under her cleated shoes was comforting. She loved the swoosh of the club as it struck the sweet spot, shooting the ball into space. The hours slipped by pleasantly, helping her put matters in perspective. This was no time to question the hurried arrest, but she knew Gibson wasn't as sure about it as she was. Or was she sure? She took out her 4-Hybrid and gave the ball a whack. It landed on the green. She forgot all about Gregory, the arrest and Gibson. After a nice dinner, she retired to bed early, exhausted from the day.

* * *

The fluorescent light flickered on grey walls smeared with despair, graffiti etched into the chipped enamel paint. Gregory sat on the lumpy bed, lumpier pillow and itchy blanket. The air inside was peculiar—fear, hate, sweat and leftover bad breath. His mind raced while his body quivered. Anguish crept over him. Down the corridor, a phone rang endlessly. Short spurts of laughter floated to his solitary chamber. In between was absolute silence. He wasn't certain which was better. He picked up on the gabble of raised voices, indiscernible words, before soft footfalls resounded on the cracked tile and halted. He caught a fleeting glimpse of a fellow turned out in a white linen suit, a Panama hat perched on wavy black hair. Gregory's eyes expanded.

"Reggie."

Reginald Pennington III snagged a chair from the far wall and lugged it over to the cell. "I understand you might need some help from a lawyer." He listed inward, slipping words of encouragement in the space between the cold steel bars. Reggie spoke in a whisper while Gregory leaned in to hear the proposal.

Chapter 14

Clouds hovered across the glacier-blue heavens. Birds wheeled in wide, lazy circles seeking thermals to stay aloft. As Eckhart sped toward the station, Gibson watched their ballet until the winged silhouettes blended into the far away sky. Their blithe freedom intensified his forlorn spirit.

"How are Cooper and Jones doing?" His voice was flat and drained.

"They're practically finished. We also hired an assistant to deal with phone calls, the mail and office stuff. She starts this week." Mischief lurked on her lips. To hell with her mother's warning.

"Good." He sank into his seat, staring off at the ever-shifting canvas of white billows in the lofty breeze.

They headed straight to the lab, swinging by the DCs who were busy setting up in the foyer, dragging cables to the office equipment. Wires blanketed the floor. The swish of the door on the tile made Frenchy look up. She dropped her eyes to the microscope, adjusting the control lever.

"It's Elsie's blood on Gregory's shirt."

Eckhart smiled.

"It merely determines that Gregory was there. Nothing further. Unless the print on the rock is his," Gibson said.

"Not quite there with the print, but I'm working hard on it," Frenchy replied, a hint of embarrassment in her voice. "Tomorrow at the latest."

"I got it." A raised voice called out from behind the partition. The technician popped up.

"Really?" Gibson turned to Frenchy.

"Oh, I meant I know what the problem is now," the technician said. His blush made his ears go pink at the tips. "There was a Trojan virus hiding in the software. I should have caught it beforehand. Sorry."

"That's okay. I know they're difficult to spot," Gibson reassured him.

"I'm cleaning everything from the computer, and then I'll do a reload. It won't be much longer." He disappeared behind the screen.

"That all sounds good to me," Gibson replied.

He turned to Eckhart. "What do you think?"

"Should we take a run out to Jacobs Landing and give Todd and Savannah the latest news about Gregory?" she asked.

"You're right. I suppose we should."

* * *

They headed out and made it to Lawsons Lane within the hour. Todd answered the door. His dishevelled appearance had improved, normalcy dangling so tantalizingly close, but his lips still quivered. Colourful, shiny brochures were dispersed across the kitchen table.

"We're making plans for the funeral." Savannah shuffled the papers around, and then shoved them all aside. "A celebration. Something simple."

Todd nodded in agreement.

"Margaret called and said Gregory—" Savannah began. She cuffed her mouth shut with the back of her hand.

"Oh. Gregory hasn't been arrested. At this point, he's only detained on his parole until we get some concrete proof," Gibson clarified.

A flicker of a smile crossed Savannah's features. She had hope that Gregory would be exonerated.

"Did anything unusual happen that day?" Gibson asked. He still wasn't convinced that Gregory had done anything other than find the body. They had no evidence against anyone yet. It was their job to keep looking. He glanced at Eckhart and saw her velvety lips harden against her teeth.

"Like what?" Todd asked.

"A quarrel with a customer? I don't know. You tell me."

"I was doing inventory in the storeroom most of the afternoon. Elsie was in the store on her own. I heard some shrieking, so I peeked in and saw her and Jackie talking. Girl stuff, I guess. Then there was a crash down one of the aisles. I was going to see what was going on, but my phone rang and I had to take it. It was a supplier. I was on the line for at least fifteen minutes. Everything was quiet by then so I went back to the inventory."

"I was at school," Savannah said flatly, kicking herself for not being any help.

Gibson didn't want to bring up the girlfriend in the middle of their funeral arrangements. He didn't have to fret about Eckhart saying anything because she believed Gregory was guilty. He would ask Todd later, after the print ID was completed.

"Didn't mean to disturb you today. We'll keep you posted," Gibson said.

"Thanks."

Savannah walked them to the front door and watched until the Expedition spun out of sight.

* * *

"We should find out what Jackie and Elsie were talking about at the store," Gibson said.

Eckhart pinched her face and rolled her eyes, but left it alone.

He dialed the Cunningham's—Jackie's mom and dad. After speaking on the phone for a few minutes, he hung up.

"They went back to BC. We'll call them later. Let's have another chat with Anatoe." He didn't think Anatoe had anything to do with the murder, but maybe Anatoe knew more than he thought he did. Gibson also had a personal motive that he was keeping to himself. He wanted another look at the guy just to make sure he was right about something unrelated to the investigation.

"I guess," Eckhart agreed, although a little begrudgingly.

"Where's his garage?"

"On Niagara Street, near downtown."

It turned out to be nearer the highway, next to a drug store. The two-storey building was aged, with red, weathered brick and a flat roof. The curtains in the top floor windows were grey and limp—Anatoe's living quarters. The ivy growing up the north side was the only greenery within ten metres of the structure. A few gnarled oak trees at the rear had endured the blacktop paving, although the leading branches were going dark and dying. The Sinclair Motors sign was nicely burnished and declared, 'We Fix Your Old Stuff'. Outside the garage door rested an older truck. In truth, it was a 1952 Ford F1, burgundy, shiny, and in mint condition. The turquoise Chevy pickup was hoisted in the air, even the underside looked immaculate.

A pair of legs with scuffed work boots on large feet stuck out from under a car in the first bay. Gibson stepped up, but before he could speak, Anatoe called out. "Give me a minute."

"It's Inspector Gibson."

The clanging ceased, and Anatoe wiggled himself out of the confined space. He scampered up, leaning backwards momentarily to stretch. A wrench dangled by his side in callused greasy palms.

"What's up?"

"Did you go to the store at Jacobs Landing on Canada Day?" Gibson asked.

"I thought Gregory was already picked up?"

"He was. But we're still asking questions."

"Yeah, I was at the store." He scratched at his temple, leaving an oil streak on his cheek.

"Did you hear or see anything surprising?"

"No."

"Were you the only one there?"

"There were a few cars out front, but nobody I knew."

"Not in the store either?"

"No, but I did overhear a quarrel between Todd and Elsie as I was leaving."

"Oh."

"I was getting a pop out of the machine. You know the old-fashioned cooler where you slide out the bottle. It's at the entrance. I was strolling down the aisle to the counter. Elsie was perched on her stool as usual when Todd stalked through from the back. He stopped when he saw me. I paid and fled. Neither one of them like me much. The door hadn't closed behind me completely when Todd started yelling. That's all I know. I didn't hear what the argument was about."

"That's fine. And then you went to Grandma's house from there?"

"That's right."

"You mentioned earlier that you got a beer from Felton's house."

"Yup."

"Anything else?" Gibson asked.

Anatoe stared into smoky eyes, his own eye twitching, and hesitated. "Someone else recognized me besides David, right?"

"Yup."

"Yeah, it was me on the landing, but it's not what you think. I wanted Elsie to know that I liked her sister. She wouldn't listen to me, so I went back to the party." He extended his palms out wide in front. "Honestly, I didn't do any—"

"You'd already had words with Elsie earlier," Gibson said.

"I wanted to sit with Savannah. Ask her out." Anatoe looked fixedly at a pothole in the asphalt.

"Is it mutual?"

"No." He rocked his head.

"So you approached Elsie repeatedly."

"Yeah, it was stupid," Anatoe admitted.

"But you didn't see or hear anyone else?" Gibson pressed on.

"No." He shuffled around. "I got to get back to work."

Gibson glanced at the burgundy truck. Anatoe tracked his gaze, his jaw shifting upwards.

"You do good work."

"Thanks."

* * *

Gibson glanced at his watch as he hopped into the truck.

"What now?" Eckhart asked.

"How about another visit to Mr. Tatlow?"

"Seriously?"

"It's all part of the puzzle. We keep plugging at it, and something will give. Trust me," he replied.

"Anatoe sounds like a lovesick puppy." She laughed.

The engine sang as Eckhart cruised up Niagara Street, down Lakeshore and over the canal to Lawsons Lane. She pulled the Expedition into Mr. Tatlow's gravelled driveway.

"It looks deserted."

"We can only try," Gibson said. He rang the bell, waited, rang again. "We're out of luck. Rats." He scanned the yard and saw some broken branches in the underbrush on the water side. "Do you think that leads to the beach? It must. Let's check it out."

Gibson pushed aside a limb, exposing a well-maintained path. He hiked to the top of the dune with Eckhart stumbling up behind him. The sun shone on the lake below, an expanse of blue with clouds reflecting on the sparkling water. They scuttled to the bottom and spilled out onto the shore, looking down on the spot where Elsie had been murdered.

"My-oh-my, does this mean anything?"

Eckhart shrugged.

"Mr. Tatlow's name has come up a few times now." Gibson wondered if the man's tragic tale had affected his judgement. He had been unduly fixated on Eckhart the past week as well. His pit-bull manner had shrivelled into a pussycat.

They sprinted up the bank.

"I say call it a day. Tomorrow could be huge."

"Yes, the print. It will tell all," Gibson said.

Eckhart swung into town. "Same time, same place."

Gibson brandished his hand backwards and entered the motel. His fascination with Eckhart was ebbing, her influence on him diminishing. He wanted to boot himself in the ass, but he went to bed early instead.

Chapter 15

White clouds, a hint of grey on the fringes, bumped into each other, gathering height in the sky. Gibson leaned against the café wall, letting the sunlight that was streaming through breaks in the darkening mass warm his skin. Seagulls were specks of silver far from the lake, free spirits gliding amid the shrinking blue. Maybe a shift in weather was coming. Gibson pressed his fingers into his tired eyes. A toot sounded from across the road. A revving of an engine nearby persisted. Finally, he released his hands and scanned the street. Eckhart had parked the Expedition in front of a fire hydrant. It vibrated on the spot. Gibson jogged over.

"Sorry, I couldn't find a space. Were you asleep standing up?"

Eckhart tapped along to a song on her steering wheel while she drove. "Frenchy called." Her speech was giddy.

"Well?"

Another titter. "She has everything ready to go."

Gibson let out a sigh.

Eckhart pulled into the parking lot and rushed to the entrance. He followed closely, trotting down the corridor.

Frenchy held the lab door open. "Get in here." She hopped on her toes. "This is just so exciting."

The DCs snuck into the room and stood in the wings.

"I got the print lifted. It was a little touch and go there for a while. But I found something that worked well," Frenchy explained.

"What substance?" Cooper asked, his eyes alight.

"Hungarian Red."

"Whoa, neat."

"The solution is exceedingly responsive to blood residue. It can recover nearly invisible latent fingerprints. Just spray on the reagent and let it dry," Frenchy continued.

The gang nodded in amazement.

"Raising the print was the risky part. I applied a gelatin lifter and drew a superb copy. Sorry it took so long, but—"

"At least we have a print to work with now. Could have all gone wrong if we'd rushed it," Gibson reassured her. "It's the only evidence we have."

"Our techie is ready too. Don't need Toronto now. Isn't that great?"

They stood in a huddle over the computer, waiting. The whirling of the hard drive was almost a purr as it spun. Gibson could feel the warmth coming off the fan. The monitor went black, and then words scrolled across the screen.

'No Match.'

"What?" Eckhart exclaimed. "That can't be. Run it again." She tugged at her locks, pushing bangs from her face. "Shit. Is it even running properly?" She shot an accusatory glare at the technician.

He hoisted his palms in defense. "It's working. There's no match." His voice was unsteady. He cleared his throat. "I could repeat it."

"Do it!" Eckhart demanded.

He punched in a round of numbers and stood upright. Gibson drew a step backward, cautiously observing the drama. The ramifications were shattering for Eckhart's theory. No fingerprint match with Gregory, no case. The DCs remained quiet, not wishing to further aggravate their boss. She was leaning into the screen, tapping on the plastic case with her long nails. Gibson could sense the vibrations emanating from her overheated body. The flush on her face had kicked up to a rouge colour. The techie bit at his fingers, willing the print to show itself. The whirring stopped. The monitor went black. The scrolling drifted across.

'No Match.'

"What the hell?" Eckhart fell into a chair. She locked eyes with Gibson. He nodded once. "Ah, crap. We have to set him free. Right?"

"I'm afraid so."

"Gregory?" Frenchy ventured.

"Yeah. We needed the print to be Gregory's if we wanted to proceed any further with him."

"Oh, that's too bad."

The technician shuffled into his corner after bearing the brunt of the blame. Frenchy moved to a microscope, twirling a knob, recalibrating the instrument.

"We'll get back to work," Cooper said as he slipped away with Jones following close behind.

"Let's go to your office and figure out our next move," Gibson suggested.

They headed down the hallway. Eckhart sat in her chair, shuffling objects around on the top of her desk. Gibson took a seat in front, plunking himself into the supple leather. The smell of newness was set free as he settled his weight into its softness. He felt like a nap. With Gregory's release, the alternatives were daunting. He considered the repercussions of murder. Always more than one casualty. The loved ones left behind hurt, passing through the stages of mourning, to hate and even revenge.

"Todd?" It was as if she had read his mind. "I can't accept that."

"We have other suspects too."

"Who? Anatoe? Mr. Tatlow?"

"And Felton," Gibson said.

"He can barely walk."

"True, but we can't rule out anyone now." Gibson got up and stood by the window, gazing at the blackened clouds. He moved back. "We'll begin with Todd," he said after merely a second's hesitation.

"Oh, boy."

A muffled ring sounded. Eckhart glanced about the office. The squawk came from the corner. "It's the landline." She jumped out of her chair and yanked open the middle drawer of a filing cabinet. Another chirp.

"Eckhart." She tugged at the tangled debris of cord and returned to her desk. "Yes, sir." She planted her elbow on top and leaned into the phone, nodding in acknowledgement. "We'll stick around." The line went dead.

"That was the superintendent. He's on his way."

"I need a coffee." Gibson stifled a yawn with his hand.

"Maybe the vending machines are functioning now. I heard some guys in the cafeteria."

"I'll go see." He surged to his feet and walked down the hallway. Cooper was on his hands and knees in the reception area. "What are you doing?"

Cooper looked up and thumped his skull on the side of the counter. "Ouch." He squatted back on his heels and smoothed the spot, a smirk passing over his features. "Connecting cables for the printer. Everything should work today."

"Great. What's Jones doing?"

"He went to get us a coffee. A team arrived to set up the cafeteria a few hours ago."

"That's where I'm headed."

"So, Gregory's out. What should we be doing?" Cooper stood up.

"You have the most important task. Maintaining the files," Gibson answered.

The constable screwed up his snout.

"There wouldn't be any convictions without chronological records. The Crown Attorney will cherish you." Gibson flashed him a quirky smile.

"What's up?" Jones asked as he sauntered in, putting two cups and several muffins on the desktop.

"Going for a coffee. Rodney is coming over," Gibson answered.

When he returned, both DCs were on the floor tearing at the wires. He stepped into the office. Eckhart was on the phone. She held up a finger. Gibson sat and sipped on his latte.

"It's Brandon." She handed over the phone.

"Hello. Eckhart told you the news." Gibson listened and responded, "Yes, we'll call them right now." He tossed the cell back. "Better get Gregory's release okayed."

She made a few more calls. A slapping of boots down the hallway alerted them to the superintendent. He swung into the room and plopped into a chair. It squealed with the onslaught. He tugged at his collar and cleared his throat. "So, we finally run the print and Gregory's out. No hit at all."

The two detectives shook their heads. Eckhart squirmed.

"What do we have?" he asked.

She offered him what they had. Nothing but suppositions and rumours. No concrete evidence.

"So, what now? We wait for someone to confess?" the superintendent said.

"We pound the pavement," Gibson replied.

"How much longer are you here?"

Gibson realized it was coming. Should he commit? He fidgeted uncomfortably. "Till the end of the weekend." Eckhart leaned in her chair and stared out the window.

"Better get at it."

At the door, the superintendent looked back. "Thanks for your assistance." He marched out.

"Ready?" Gibson pitched his paper cup into the garbage pail.

"Yup." She left hers on the desk still half-full.

* * *

The drive to Lawsons Lane was uneventful. Eckhart refrained from drumming on the steering wheel. Gibson sprawled out and stared out the side window. The tires hummed over the grate on the bridge. He appreciated the mesmerizing sound. No ships in either direction, but in the far-off distance, a trail of black smoke drifted from Lock Two in the south. She veered left at the final intersection.

"Take us to the beach access first."

Eckhart flipped him a quizzical expression, lines appearing between her eyebrows. She drew to the grassy shoulder at the end of the lane and clicked off the ignition. They remained for several minutes. He looked at the landing, not disclosing his thoughts. The Expedition creaked as the motor cooled down. Finally, he glanced at Eckhart and said, "We don't have a handle on the motive yet. What about opportunity?"

Eckhart smoothed her hair from her forehead and faced him. She forced her lips together, sick of going over and over the same material. "We know Anatoe was there. And Mr. Tatlow." She paused. "What are you thinking?"

"There was one other individual there?"

"Who?"

"David," Gibson said.

"Oh, I suppose."

"He told us he was."

"Yeah." Eckhart tucked her legs up and wiggled around until she confronted him full on.

"So, if we accept Anatoe went back to the house and Mr. Tatlow left..." Gibson said, pausing for effect. "Did David return to the party? Or did he follow Elsie down the steps? Did he have time?"

Eckhart gasped. "Whoa. But here comes the why again."

"Why? If we could answer that..." Gibson trailed off and shifted in his seat. "No. Let's stick with Todd for the time being. We should find out what kind of person Elsie was. Todd cheated on her. And where was he during the fireworks? There's more to understand." He swivelled back. They locked eyes. Her deep pools of blue still haunting him, but losing ground.

Eckhart fired up the truck, made a one-eighty and headed to the top of the lane. The store looked desolate and uncared for. Gibson went down the path with his thoughts in a muddle. Eckhart's springy step was gone as well. Todd's vehicle sat in the driveway, a film of dirt glued to the windshield. Todd answered the door dressed in rumpled polyester pants and a pale blue shirt. He crept down the corridor to the living room with his slippers flopping, flinging dust bunnies along the baseboards. The pallor of his skin had altered somewhat, two pecks of pink showed on his cheeks. He hurled himself onto the couch and sunk into the cushions. "The funeral is in a few days." He held back the tears, lashes stuck together from crying. His gesture swept the room.

"What's this all for?"

Gibson sat in a chair by the unlit fireplace. Eckhart settled into a spot adjacent to Todd. The clicking of her fingernails echoed throughout the space.

"Did you murder Elsie?" Gibson saw no other course. The abruptness made Todd thrust back into the seat.

"What? No. I thought they arrested Gregory."

"We've released him," Gibson said. "Did you—"

"How could you suggest that?" he cut in. A solitary tear rolled from his inflamed eyes and slid down to his chin. He swept at it absently. There was an ache to his stillness, his hands clenching into fists. No sound left his trembling lips, just the heaving of his chest as he fought for air.

Gibson locked his smoky greys onto Todd's lifeless eyes. Eckhart cringed. Here it comes. She clamped her mouth as Gibson spewed the nasty.

"We met Josephine. JoJo, if you like."

Todd's ears rang hollow. The room dimmed. He descended into its fervor. It spat him out, hurling him into the outstretched arms of his betrayal. His lie exposed. He blinked. More tears traced down his colourless face, the two spots of pink having fled.

"It's—" Eckhart began, but was instantly shut down by a glower from Gibson. She covered her mouth and watched grief destroy the man.

Gibson's face stiffened into a somber expression. He delayed. The pit-bull inside him fixed to bark, to bite.

"Todd," he said sharply.

Todd rubbed at his forehead. His gaze flitted around the room. His mouth twitched. "It was just once. A mistake." He groaned.

Gibson let the silence linger. The pit-bull put his hackles down.

"I went to Grimsby to confront Anatoe," he finally said, raising his head, mournful eyes beseeching.

Gibson remained distant.

"I wouldn't hurt my wife. I love Elsie," Todd said.

"Did she find out about your adventure?"

"No." He winced at the remark.

"What happened when you didn't call up or come home?"

"I phoned her." His voice lifted an octave higher. He blathered on. "I told her I'd had too much to drink and couldn't drive. I would stay with a cousin of Anatoe."

"How did that go over?" Gibson pushed. "Elsie detested Anatoe."

"Not real well." Todd collapsed into himself, hands massaging his thighs.

"So, no argument when you made it home?"

"No. I brought her chocolates. Her favourite." He wept softly.

"You told us you weren't at the fireworks. Where were you?" A clipped voice spat out the question.

"I was at the store. I already told you." Todd paused. "Doing the books. I never saw Elsie. I arrived at the party, but she was gone."

Back to Grimsby. "What did you tell Anatoe?" Gibson asked next.

"What? When?"

"When you went to Grimsby."

"I needed Anatoe to leave Savannah alone. He wasn't good enough for her."

"Okay," Gibson said.

"And to quit jeering at my wife. She's not fat." Todd stifled the next sob.

"Did you threaten him?"

"No."

"Did you know Anatoe overheard the quarrel between you and Elsie that afternoon?"

Todd's eyes sprung wide, further tears tumbled out.

"You were yelling."

Todd shook his head in denial.

Gibson pressed his lips into a frown. Eckhart stared at the ceiling.

"Elsie was spreading hearsay again. Still. I've told her a thousand times to stop." He gagged on his words.

"Who was she talking to?"

"Jackie. I wasn't lying about that."

"I understand. So their chatter was more than a happy-to-see-you."

Todd nodded.

"What was it about then?" Gibson wanted clarity.

"It was about Gregory and his release from prison. That part was true, but she said he would do it again. She should have left it alone." He drew his breath in. "Gregory was another guy Elsie didn't care for. Guess nobody was good enough for her little sister. I didn't know then that Savannah liked Gregory." He shrugged. "It's Savannah's mistake, not my problem."

"Is that all you heard?"

"Yeah. Elsie went on and on about it. I warned her gossiping would get her into trouble one day. She..." Todd choked.

"Who else was in the store?"

"I'm not sure. Oh, Mr. Tatlow came in at his usual time." He stopped. "There was a crash. Okay. I told you that." Todd was getting confused. "That's all I know. I'm not lying." Shame and anger burned in his heart. He filled the vacuum with heaving sobs for his new reality. He didn't try to check the burst dam, but let his grief surge into a roaring river, sweeping everything in its path.

Gibson pointed his chin at Eckhart. Her legs buckled when she stood, besieged by Todd's misery. He grabbed at her arm. No electricity passed this time. Relief rushed through him. An easy smile flitted across his lips. Eckhart tugged at her hair. "I'm okay."

They slipped out of the house, anguish following them down the sidewalk into their own fears.

* * *

The walls were greyer than yesterday. Or was it his mood? Gregory turned on the flimsy mattress, crushed by his hefty frame, cold seeping into his bones. He opened and closed his eyes. No. Still in the hellhole. Breakfast was regurgitating in his throat. He swallowed to keep it down. The damn phone had sounded all night. The lights strobed in the corridor. Even the sweater stretched over his face didn't stop the incessant flicker. Reggie had been nice, but he was nevertheless in lockup. Four days, three nights, seventy-four hours... at a guess. Keys jangled from a tight belt around a loose body. Shuffled footsteps. Other shoes, hurried ones, clicked on the linoleum. Gregory sat up, nudging aside the useless blanket. He clawed at his itchy arms. Was it lunch already? Two smiling faces peeped through the bars. A guard moved up from behind, sifting through a ring of keys. With a broad indication of his hand, he held up the one that would give Gregory his freedom.

Brandon smirked. Reggie put a finger to his lips. Silence. "Let's get out of here."

Gregory jogged down the long hallway and out into the sunshine, squinting his eyes against the welcome assault. He howled. "Is it over?"

"Yes." They hopped into Reggie's Range Rover and flew away.

Chapter 16

Savannah sat cross-legged in the midst of the marram grass that topped the dunes, listening to the lullaby of waves breaking on the shore below. The sun began the morning with flashes peeking from the east. It had risen higher now, the brilliance and warmth scattering through a navy sky. A sandspit ran out and reached for the shoreline across the modest basin. A lighthouse, solitary and abandoned, dazzled white against the placid water, paler blue than the dome above. Dogs frolicked down the beach flicking sand behind their rushing paws. Owners whistled and barked to rein them in. Not likely. Savannah laughed at their antics.

Gregory scampered up the path from his father's property adjoining the waterfront. The bluff overlooking the lake encapsulated his fondness of nature. He inhaled the tang of faraway continents. Savannah waved him over from her partial screen behind the tallest grasses. He hurried over, his footsteps sinking in the silky sand, and hunkered down beside her. Beyond, the coast rendered a thin, dark line. In the clean light of the morning, they could see black skyscrapers battling the smog. Farther in the distance, the land swooped out of view.

Savannah loved this beach. She struggled not to think about Elsie lying lifeless at the bottom of the steps. Whatever the evil was, she was resolved it would not take away all she cherished. She glimpsed at Gregory. His strong jaw and passionate eyes carried a pledge of integrity. She knew he grappled with his loss of freedom. Savannah forced back the tears of her own grief for her sister.

* * *

The hiss of traffic obscured the strangled ringing. Jackie paused and tipped her head, trying to distinguish the noise. The landline. She tripped over the last step and bounded to the landing. After a harried rummaging in her purse, she plucked out a loop with too many keys attached. As she fumbled to get the correct one, the high-pitched sound ceased. "Oh, shit." She squared her shoulders and stuck the key into the lock. The phone spat out another round of annoyance. She elbowed the door wide, banging it against the wall and raced down the corridor. What could be so urgent?

"Hello," Jackie answered somewhat stiffly, almost insolently.

"It's your mother. Your dad is in the hospital. He's had a heart attack." Her mother's strained speech snapped out the words.

"Will he be all right?" She put her palm on her chest. Fear stabbed at her ribs and made her mouth parched.

"Just get here."

"Okay," Jackie said.

"Good." Her mom hung up before she could respond.

Jackie slid into the recliner, still clinging to the dead phone and wept. Frustration boiled into a quiet rage. She pounded her fists on her thighs and booted the coffee table. A thin laughter whistled through her pinched lips. She sagged further into the cushion, running her fingers along the frayed piping. The bitterness ebbed as she worked the fabric. She let the rise and fall of her chest slow her breathing. Time to make a move. She rose and marched to the home office. With a few clicks on the keyboard, she booked herself on an overnight flight. Although they had been back a number of days, Jackie hadn't unpacked her suitcase so she threw in some clean underclothes and a toothbrush. As she snapped the lid shut, she heard a rattle. That would be David coming home from work. Jackie had one last look around, grabbed her bag and dashed to the front. David stepped back, startled as someone snatched the door from his grip. She wavered in the entryway, soft strands of hair swept past an ear. Her dark lashes brimmed with silvery tears. A case stood by her side.

"I have to go."

"What?"

"Tonight. Now. My dad."

Jackie pushed past him with the bag in hand. David locked the door and rushed to catch up. It was a quick trip to the airport on newly paved roads. The glass and concrete building reflected light from a sun perched at the tip of the central airstrip, just about to dip below the mountains. They sprinted from the short-term parking to the entrance. There was barely anyone in the terminal. Jackie hoped she hadn't missed her flight. At the counter, she turned toward David and threw him a kiss.

"I'll let you know what's happening." And then she disappeared through sliding glass doors.

* * *

The tires squealed as they struck and rebounded off the tarmac. Jackie stared through the tiny pane as the plane coasted down the runway to where they would disembark. The clouds had cleared out, the threat of rain abated in the transparent blueness. The early glimmers of light dropped through the buildings in the east and washed on the windows of the control tower.

Jackie bounded to the arrivals gate and snatched the first car. After a long ride from Toronto, the Uber driver pulled into the darkened cul-de-sac. She could see the silhouette of her mom standing in the bay window. A light from an upstairs pane shone over the neighbour's blank wall. She swept her palm on her father's car as she went by. Her mom swung the door open to greet her, and they headed to the kitchen. Cups littered the countertop as if all they served here was tea.

"Is Dad going to make it?" Jackie asked.

"I hope so," her mom answered and switched to a less painful topic seamlessly. "The detectives phoned here."

"Why?"

"They had more questions about the incident."

"Like what?" Jackie asked.

"Who was at the store that day?"

"What about Gregory? I thought he was arrested for the…" She stopped at the next word, not allowing herself to say it.

"Beats me. But they were anxious to talk to you and David again."

"Okay. Eckhart left me a couple of messages, but I didn't phone back yet."

"I guess you better," her mom replied.

"Yeah, I will."

Jackie slipped out of the room and headed to the washroom downstairs to freshen up. The twittering of birds as they swooped from branch to branch in pursuit of unsuspecting bugs, floated in from an open window. A sublime light shone through the wooden slates saturating the room with warmth. She went into the family room and stopped in front of her father's favourite spot on the couch. The indentation in the cushion was permanent. Now she understood he was not. The tear rolled down her cheek before she could check it. Mom had turned the radio on, but even that noise didn't fill the emptiness of the house without her dad in it. Her thoughts floated back to Elsie again. Would that pain never stop?

The hospital was a four-storey brick building designed in a u-shape so many of the rooms faced onto a courtyard. Gigantic old elms and maples from the turn of the century dotted the well-tended gardens. Cobblestone paths meandered through a rose bed to a pagoda.

Jackie rode the elevator to her dad's suite and stuck her head in the doorway. A frail ashen face peeped out from cotton sheets.

"Dad."

A smile filled the hollows of his sunken cheeks. Jackie balanced on the edge of the narrow bed, glancing at the green walls—the colour of wilted spinach. There wasn't a picture or decoration in sight, just mind-numbing blankness. Jackie talked while Dad lay back on the pillows and listened. A soft knock on the doorframe stopped their conversation.

"Hi, Reggie. Have a seat." Her dad pointed to the solitary chair left in the corner. He tugged his fatigued body further up in the bed, wrenching on the tubes and wires attached to his right arm. His other hand shot up to ward off help.

"Nice to see you, Reg," Jackie said. They had been friends since high school, more than friends. He had done well, graduating with a law degree.

"Any word about what's going on? My mom said Eckhart wanted to talk to me."

"Gregory has been released," Reggie answered.

"What? How do you know?"

"I'm his lawyer. He's no longer a suspect." Reggie smiled.

"Oh, so that explains it. Guess I better phone then. Although I'm not sure what I could tell them," Jackie said.

"They obviously have a lead on something," he answered.

They settled into a pleasant discussion and before long an hour had passed by. Her dad slumped down, his pjs riding up to his chin. His eyes wavered, flickered and shut. A snore escaped his soft mouth, and peace settled over his dull features.

"Time to go." Jackie brushed her lips on her dad's cool skin and shuddered. As they walked out of the room, her cell phone rang.

* * *

Gloom swirled around Gibson when he first woke. The artificial glow of street lamps trickled into the room past the heavy curtains he had neglected to shut. He got up and showered. Billows of steam wafted out of the open bathroom door, fogging all the mirrors and windows. He lingered under the scalding water cascading over his lean frame.

Gibson dressed, suppressing his inclination to tune out. As he stepped outside, indigo skies brought warmth to his core. It astonished him how many tones of blue the heavens could grant. With a lighter tread, he made his way to the café. He sat at the window observing the traffic stream by—a blast of a horn, a screech of tires and a few choice words. A sweet, earthy scent drifted to his snout as a professional woman scraped by, reminding him of Katherine. Why hadn't she answered her phone last night? Or this morning? He stared off in a stupor until a string of toots caught his awareness. An idling Expedition was framed in the huge picture window, halfway on the walk, jamming traffic on both the road and the sidewalk. Gibson jumped up, tossed bills on the table and ran to the vehicle.

"What the hell." Eckhart clipped at him. "Duh."

"Sorry. Didn't see you."

"What's up for today?"

"We have to keep pushing. Something will click." He peered at her. "Did you hear from Jackie or David yet?"

"No. I left two messages."

"Mm."

"Where am I going?"

"Lawsons Lane. That's where the crime took place. The answers are there," Gibson said with conviction. "But let's stop at Anatoe's garage first."

"Do you think he knows more?"

Gibson made a noise of acknowledgement, his thoughts already on another path.

She tilted her head to the side, lines forming between her eyebrows. "Are you thinking he makes a good suspect?"

"Not really." His shoulders rose so vaguely the gesture was almost indiscernible.

She took fringe streets and cut across major routes to dodge the rush hour. She tore up to the garage doors of Sinclair Motors, but they were closed, locked up tight. She looked up to the second-floor windows, but there was no light or motion there either. "Where's he gone? He had lots of work the other day."

Gibson reached into his pocket and yanked out his cell. He glanced at the number on the sign above the door and dialed. While he waited for an answer, he said, "Maybe Anatoe has call forwarding." He hung up on the tenth ring. "Guess not."

Eckhart backed out of the property and headed north. The traffic had scattered so it was easy going now. They hit the bridge in twenty minutes, humming across the metallic surface. Gibson saw a flock of birds circling at the stern of a departing ship in the distance. He could just make out a lone figure flinging stuff out of a bucket into the canal. The gulls dived into the churning waters, coming up with full beaks of something. It was too far away to tell.

A trail of brown grunge flew out behind the truck as Eckhart careened down the lane. It swirled in huge whiffs, and then flattened into a sheet, extending out past the ditches into the fields. She ignored the dust storm she had created and crunched to a standstill in the Tatlow driveway.

"Doesn't look like anybody's home. What do you think?"

"Let's go see," she answered.

Gibson rang the bell and waited for an answer. He peered through a window, but the curtains were closed. He pressed on the bell again.

"Where has everyone gone?"

Gibson twisted his mouth into a frown.

"I'm not sure how I feel about Mr. Tatlow. Are we missing something?" Gibson mused. He stared at the camouflaged entry to the beach. "We should go back to Felton's house."

"Why? We've cleared Gregory. Although…" Eckhart had really wanted it to be him. Her first case closed, but it wasn't to be.

"I've been thinking about the paths from the beach. I think there's one at his place."

"How will that help?"

"Felton or someone else could have slipped from the yard, bustled down to the waterfront and—"

"Gotten back to the party. Nobody the wiser," Eckhart finished his sentence.

"Exactly," Gibson said.

Eckhart turned the Expedition around in the wide driveway and headed across the street. She drove past the pump house and pulled in next to Felton's vehicle. Gregory's motorbike was missing. An occasional pop of yellow stood out amongst the green in the dahlia bed. They strode to the front veranda in companionable silence. From behind the screen door, they heard low voices. Gibson gestured to Eckhart. She stopped on the bottom step as he marched up to the door. He rapped on the wooden frame. "Hello there. It's Gibson."

"What the hell do you want with us already? Haven't you done enough?" Felton yelled.

"We have nothing more to say." Margaret pushed the flimsy door open and stepped out. "I have my family back." She stood with hands on hips, chin jutted out.

Her husband shoved his face into the mesh, looking surly. He stared hard at the inspector and then narrowed his eyes. "That's all that matters. So leave us alone."

Gibson backed up, almost tripping on the top stair. "We don't mean to bother you. Just checking out beach accesses."

Felton cleared his throat, sending him into a coughing fit. He pulled out his dirty handkerchief and spat. Margaret glared at him. He waved a hand in dismissal. "Fill your boots," he said to Gibson. "There's a path in the corner."

"Thanks." Gibson thought of something else and looked back. "Does everybody here know about the footpath?"

"I guess." He shrugged and hobbled out of sight. A scuffling sound drifted out of the doorway. Felton struggling with his lame leg?

Gibson bounded away before Margaret yammered more crap. He hurried round the house to the rear, Eckhart rushing along beside him. They passed the fireworks pit. Gibson stopped and turned in a circle with his eyes scanning the yard. From here, he couldn't see the front lawn where the partygoers had hung out. His thoughts raced. They continued and found the path. Not hidden, as Mr. Tatlow's was. It was steeper though. They scampered to the top. Grasses covered most of the area but gave a clear view over the lake. They slipped down the other side.

"That was a challenge," Eckhart said.

Gibson looked back up. They plodded through the sand, dodging the mass of logs piled at the bottom of the dunes. It took only minutes to get to the stairs and the crime scene.

"Oh boy."
"Yeah?"

"Anybody could have come over that bluff and…" He drew his mouth into a straight line and bit his lip. "Damn." There were several people without an alibi.

"Crap." Her scrunched-up face showed the frustration.

They trudged up the stairs and spun left to retrieve the truck. Gibson turned to see Margaret standing on the veranda, staring them off the property as they crept out of the driveway. Eckhart drove slower up the lane, leaving the dust in its place. At the stop sign, she waited for the traffic to go barrelling through. Gibson's gaze swung over to Jacobs Landing. Someone had covered the windows with graffiti. He lowered his head and groaned.

"What?"

He pointed to the store.

"Oh shit. That's a lousy thing to do," she said. "Where to now?"

Gibson pulled his cell from his back pocket, struggling against his seatbelt. He threw Eckhart an odd smile. She glanced at his tight jeans and smiled in return.

He dialed Abigail, Jackie's mom. It rang several times before she answered, wheezing down the line. "Sorry, I was downstairs."

"We've been trying to reach Jackie. She doesn't answer her cell. Does she have a home phone?"

"Yes, but she flew back to see her dad. He's in hospital."

"I see. Maybe give me her number again."

It was the same number. After Gibson rang off, he tried to call Jackie again. She answered right away.

"We have some questions for you. Could we pick you up?" he asked.

"Just a sec."

He heard some commotion in the background and waited. Jackie came back on the line. "I'll come over to the office if that is okay. How about in a half hour?"

"That would be good."

He gave her directions and disconnected the call before she could change her mind.

"Jackie is meeting us at the office."

"Sounds good." Eckhart drove down the road at a quick pace, then stomped on the accelerator when they approached the canal. The truck leaped over the metal grating. The ship on Gibson's side was scary large, right in his face.

"What the hell?" He plunged back into the bucket seat, snagging the handhold.

Sirens sounded behind them and lights flashed. The road barrier slammed into place. Gibson turned in his chair and watched the bridge lift into the sky.

"We nearly got trapped." Her shriek was boisterous and throaty. The growl of the engine eased as she braked to a cruising speed. Gibson wilted into the leather and tuned in to the tires singing on the country road. Eckhart fiddled with the radio, deciding on soft rock. She headed along Lakeshore Road into Port Dalhousie, past her apartment, and came to a halt at the station. "How is Jackie getting here?"

"I'm not sure."

A Lincoln Continental pulled in beside them. The blue paint revealed a mention of wine in the brilliant sunlight like a buried jewel. Classy.

"Wow. Didn't think Mr. Cunningham would let anyone drive it," Eckhart remarked.

Jackie exited the car, sandaled feet with pastel pink toenails touching the ground first. Long bronze legs followed. She glanced at the detectives. The sun sparked her green eyes, yielding a deep shade of forest, playing tricks with the daylight just as the Lincoln had.

"Hi."

"Thanks for coming," Gibson said.

Eckhart unlocked the entry with her card key and advanced inside to silence. She walked through the empty detective agency, heels clicking on the tile, and opened the door to her office. It wasn't a huge room, but it was comfortable. Gibson followed her, Jackie tagging in his wake. Eckhart leaned against the window frame, gesturing with her hand. Gibson stepped up to the desk and pointed to the single chair in front. Jackie sat balanced on the rim of the cushion, legs crossed and fingers interlaced over one knee. He established his elbows on the oak surface, hands touching palm to palm in prayer poise and leaned forward. Eckhart turned and peered out the window, engaged by the slight summer wind catching the foliage of the maples. It fashioned a sequence of brightness and shadow on the lawn.

"In case you haven't heard, Gregory has been released. He is no longer a suspect," Gibson said. He detected a muted raise of Jackie's eyebrows and continued, "You were at the store that morning."

"I wanted to say hi to Savannah, but she wasn't there," Jackie answered.

"But you spoke to Elsie."

Her mouth opened, but no sound came out. Her lips trembled.

Gibson nodded and got down to business. "What time did you get there?"

"Late in the afternoon. We had just flown in from Victoria."

"You and David."

"Yes, but David waited in the car for me."

"So, tell me what happened when you went in."

"I went to the counter where Elsie was sitting," Jackie started, letting out a huge sigh. "She was leaning over a newspaper, the daily, and didn't notice me arrive at first. We hugged, and then I sat on a stool across from her."

"What happened next?"

"We chatted."

"About what?"

"She was ranting about Gregory getting parole. But I already knew that," Jackie said.

"From whom?"

"My mom had told me. Gregory and I kind of grew up together. In the summer, I went to my grandma's place next door."

"What else did you talk about?"

"Well, Elsie does ramble on, so I sort of zoned out. She gossips a lot, and I was thinking about other stuff. You know, my dad being sick. Anyway, I heard her say 'like father, like son'."

Gibson leaned in further. "Who was she talking about?"

Jackie shrugged.

"Do you think she was still talking about Gregory?" he pressed on.

"I suppose she could have been. Maybe Felton got into trouble too when he was young. Although I don't believe Gregory did what they said. It doesn't sit right with me."

"Did Elsie say anything else?"

"Something about the beach," Jackie stopped. "No, it was not at the beach. Yeah, that's what she said. It was not at the beach. Whatever that means? Maybe she was talking about the fireworks that evening being at Felton's place, not on the beach. I'm sorry. It could have been anything. Then I heard a box or something tumble to the floor at the front of the store and a loud bang of a door at the back. And if that didn't startle me enough, that creepy Mr. Tatlow showed up. His piercing eyes gave me nightmares when I was a kid. Still do." She blasted out a gigantic breath.

Something niggled. Gibson couldn't quite place it, like a word on the tip of your tongue, and you couldn't spit it out. So he let it pass.

"Did anyone else come in after that?"

"A few people that I didn't know. A young girl getting smokes. Some kids were hanging out by the magazines." Jackie's olive skin had paled. She wiped stray tears away from her eyes. "Sorry. It's just my friend and my dad."

"Don't be sorry."

"Family is so important. It's easy to forget," Jackie said. Her emerald eyes turned a wild green like an ocean in a tempest.

Gibson glanced down and thought about his family. A clamor in the corridor broke the spell. A door slammed and the clomping of boots on the hard floors echoed into the office. He didn't raise his head at the sound of approaching footsteps.

Cooper rolled up to the doorway. "Hey. Coffee anybody?" He stopped. "Oops. Didn't realize you had someone here." He withdrew into the corridor.

"It's okay. No coffee for me," Gibson shouted after him. He had already had his fill for the day and didn't need another jolt to his frazzled nerves. He stared at the ladies. "Yes, no?"

Eckhart brandished her hand in a big no.

"No." Jackie jumped out of her chair. "Are we done?"

"Yes. Thanks for your help. Are you okay?" His smoky eyes presented the unease he felt.

"I'm fine. I hope you get the killer. Elsie didn't deserve..."

Jackie struggled to stem the downhill plunge. The sadness robbed her of the person she had formerly been. She chewed her lip, keeping in the deluge of tears that had been menacing since she landed in town. Gibson moved from behind the desk and placed his arm around her shoulders. He escorted her across the central foyer and released the door. A sultry breeze swirled in.

"Another heatwave is growing."

"I think you're right." Some colour flooded into her honey brown complexion.

"Take care," Gibson said.

Jackie climbed into the Lincoln and fired up the big V8. She hustled down the lane like there was no tomorrow. Maybe there wasn't for her. Her eyes welled up. No one to witness her pain streaming down her cheeks now.

Eckhart swung back to the window, her gaze concentrated on the maples again. Gibson entered, the prance lost in his stride. He perched in the lone chair Jackie had occupied.

"We need to talk to David. He had a front-row seat of everyone coming and going from the store. Although I'm not sure where this is going yet." Gibson rang the number that Jackie had given him. He shook his head and left a message.

"Why don't people answer their cell phones?" Eckhart asked.

"There's something, however," Gibson mused.

"What?"

"So much death on Lawsons Lane."

"Huh?"

"It's just an idea. We should check it out." His gaze darkened, and he looked out the window. They remained in silence for a few minutes. Gibson stood up and went to the doorway. He called out, "Cooper. Get in here."

The DC scooted down the corridor almost knocking Gibson flat. "Oops."

Gibson clapped him on the upper arm and winked. "I have a project for you."

Cooper's face lit up.

"Jones can lend a hand."

"Okay." Cooper waited.

"Katie Underwood. The child that drowned at the beach on Lawsons Lane—"

"Yeah," Cooper interrupted.

Gibson tightened his eyes. "Hold on. Could you locate her file? You may have to dig around. It was years ago."

"How does any of that tally into this?" Eckhart asked, her pouting lips pink and full.

"Not really sure. Probably doesn't. But it bothers me when more than one suspicious death happens on a street. Especially when they all know each other."

"I guess," Eckhart said.

Cooper bounced on his feet, swinging from side to side as if he was expecting a gun to signal the launch of a marathon. He didn't barge in again, but compressed his lips together.

"Okay, Cooper. Maybe the superintendent can confirm where the files are. Who knows if they are digital or paper?" Gibson stopped. "Come to think about it. There was another death. Two actually."

"What are you talking about?" Eckhart exclaimed.

"Mr. Tatlow. His wife and child died? Who knows? Are the deaths connected?"

"That's stretching it, don't you think?" she asked, giving him a funny look.

"Maybe." Gibson shrugged and turned to Cooper. "Any questions?"

"No." The DC sprung off the balls of his feet and sprinted to his partner's office. His voice reverberated around the building.

"What a case," Eckhart said.

"If nothing else, it will be good practice for them," Gibson replied and glanced out the window.

Chapter 17

The sun had barely risen and was already chasing the coolness of the night away. Gibson walked down the street with his head bowed, feeling thwarted. A trill of a lone bird made him glance upward. The feathered lover sat on the rim of a hanging basket calling for its mate. Maybe there was a nest concealed in the flowers. The blossoms reminded him of his home on the island. Spring in Victoria brought the robins, the rufous hummingbirds and 1,600 flower baskets suspended from the lampposts. Hence the city's nickname—City of Gardens. He dragged his heels on a pavement that would be scorched by noon. The café was packed this morning, a sign of a hectic weekend ahead. He grabbed a coffee and moved outside to wait for his ride. The Expedition crept stealthily around the corner and bolted the curb. He hopped into the truck and slumped into the seat. Eckhart glimpsed over, humming faintly and tapping the steering wheel.

"Cooper called. He has some info for us."

"Already."

"He's a keeper." Her voice was bubbly.

It was a twelve-minute drive to the office. Gibson watched the endless expanse of flatness. His hometown comprised of mountains, infinite ocean and forest. He gazed into the distance with a vague longing. The truck jerked to a halt.

"Sorry." Her eyes crinkled, deepening the creases in the corners.

The large steel door lurched open as they approached the station. Cooper's towering figure was straight and proud, holding up a binder for them to see. A pleasant glow flushed his cheeks. Then his hand dropped to his side along with his grin, thinking maybe he had jumped the gun.

"I found the info, but I'm not sure it'll help," Cooper said as his posture sagged.

"Let's see." Gibson reached out for the folder.

They strode inside, barring the surging heat out.

A girl bounded into the foyer from the lunchroom, headphones hooked over her ears and a ponytail swaying with her gait. Her complexion was flawless, like many young women who stayed out of the sun. She wore Bermuda shorts with a tight T-shirt and red running shoes that squealed on the tile when she stopped abruptly.

"Oh, hello. I'm Daisy. The receptionist."

She grinned and scrutinized Gibson's lean frame, his un-bleached sandy hair, a mere hint of grey, and smoky eyes.

"Gibson. Pleased to meet you."

The phone sounded from somewhere above. Daisy pressed a button on her headset with neatly trimmed nails and returned to her post at the receptionist counter. "Niagara Task Force."

Gibson looked around the entrance hall for Cooper, but he had disappeared. Eckhart motioned to the offices at the end of the corridor. The DC was behind his desk, waving them in. They sat in straight-backed chairs with cushioned seats. Gibson placed the folder on the top and flipped it open. Eckhart leaned in to steal a peek. He nudged it over so they could both read. It didn't take long. There were only six pages.

"This is the entire inquiry?" Gibson was hoping he didn't sound condescending.

"I'm afraid so." Cooper coughed to clear his throat. "The detectives on the Katie Underwood case never suspected foul play. It was declared an accidental drowning right from the start."

He drummed his palm on the file.

"The girls were on the beach and left their bikes on the landing as they usually did. Savannah and Jackie left for lunch. Katie stayed to inspect a frog or something. That's not definite. They were just scared kids. Not really sure what was going on, I suspect. Anyway, her mom got concerned when Katie didn't appear by one o'clock, more than an hour past lunchtime. Mrs. Underwood phoned over to the store, but her daughter wasn't there. Then she went hunting down the street for Katie and found her bike at the top of the stairs. She figured Katie was on the beach and had headed down to the shore. But there was no trace of her anywhere. After a few hours, Mrs. Underwood realized Katie was gone."

Cooper hesitated and blew out air. He had pretty well recited the article verbatim.

"That's when she called the police. The search and rescue team dragged the bay for her body, but there are undertows here and there. In the end, the detectives figured she just went out too far and got caught in an undertow." Cooper trailed his finger down the final sheet. "There's a description of her garments. Blue shorts, white and blue striped top, and sandals."

"Did you ring the lead detective?" Gibson tapped the folder.

"Harry something. I forget. Anyway, he died a few years ago. Heart attack," Cooper answered.

"Nothing else?"

Cooper shook his head.

"That's okay. Elimination is as important as finding things. Right?"

"I suppose."

"What about Mr. Tatlow? Did you find anything there?"

"No. There was never an investigation, but I went to the hospital and rifled through a ton of paperwork. I didn't have a date to start with. But there aren't that many infant deaths, so I found the file fairly quickly. His wife died in childbirth. No funny business."

"Well, it was a long shot. I'm just looking for people connections." Gibson wasn't sure how any of it would have fitted in, but he had been surprised before. He looked around the office. "I see you guys are prepared to rock and roll now. Great set up."

"Yes. We are. Because of you," Eckhart said, her voice warm with appreciation. She smiled at Gibson.

"No problem. I—" His phone chirped. He checked the screen and held up a finger. Oh good. "Hi, David. I'm with Inspector Eckhart and DC Cooper. I'm putting you on speaker." Gibson fumbled with the buttons. A buzz sounded, and they could hear David breathing down the line. Gibson arranged the cell on the desk and hunched forward.

"Okay. Thanks for calling," Gibson said. "On the afternoon of the fireworks, I understand you and Jackie stopped at Jacobs Landing."

"Yeah, we did."

"And you sat in the car while Jackie went inside."

"Yeah."

"Were you watching who was coming and going?"

"Sure, I guess I was. But I'm not from around here so I didn't really know anyone," David answered.

"Okay. Tell me what you can," Gibson said.

"The first person I saw was this old man. He had the creepiest eyes. I've never seen anything like it. They were pure black and freaky looking. He went in the store right after Jackie did. Later I found out that was Mr. Tatlow. Apparently, he's well known around here, lives by the beach. Then, after a few minutes, an old woman in a straw hat left the store and headed down the lane. Mr. Tatlow came out of the store right behind her and went down the lane as well. There were a few other people that I can't remember much about. But then a nice turquoise pickup pulled into the parking lot. Of course, I know now that was Anatoe. Then Jackie returned and we left."

"That's it? A few more details would be helpful," Gibson said.

"What? Did you want me to write up a report or something? Nobody rushed out with a bloody knife," David yelled, emitting a scornful sound.

No one spoke.

"Oh, that was lousy of me. I don't know why I said that. But how many times can I go through this?"

"Don't worry about it. We're all feeling tense," Gibson answered. He kept forgetting that David's boss had been murdered last year. Give him a break. "If you think of anything else. No matter how trivial it seems, call me."

"Sure. Sorry. I really am."

"Thanks for your help."

David hung up without retorting. The speakerphone droned for a time before he punched a button and silence gripped the room.

"Let's have lunch."

"You guys did well," Gibson said and extended the DC a fist pump.

"Thanks." Cooper collapsed into the leather seat, intertwining his fingers behind his neck and gazed at the ceiling with a plucky grin smeared around his features.

"I'm taking you to the Skyline," Eckhart announced. When they walked out of the office, Daisy was on the phone so they chopped her a salute.

A sweltering heat pushed in when Gibson swung the door open. "Whoa. It's hardly past noon."

They plunged into the blaze of brightness. The Iris skies had dulled to a paler rendering of blue. Even the birds were subdued. They headed out of town. Gibson relaxed, unfolding his legs in front, always ready to stretch out his tall frame. Eckhart raised the volume of the radio to one notch below annoying. The roads spread in all angles, from the escarpment to the lake and overflowing into the next town. The suburban sprawl bumped into the vineyards that had sprung up over the last decade. Once they struck the Queen Elizabeth Highway, it was easy sailing to Niagara Falls. Eckhart meandered through the boulevards when they hit town, but parked in a no-parking zone nonetheless, her normal MO. They hastened to the relative cool of the glass and steel lobby and jetted to the top of the tower in a box of white marble walls and a grey tile floor. As Gibson stepped out of the elevator, he collided into the last person he expected to see—Arthur Brockelman. He stroked his crooked snout, recalling in that instant the tussle with Katherine's ex-husband.

The bloke stared hard at him, his eyes taking on a lethal edge. His hands bunched into fists at his side, ready for a tumble. After only a moment's pause, he snarled, "Gibson."

"Brockelman." Gibson pressed his lips together. They remained in limbo, Eckhart wavering in the background.

Arthur's young companion twiddled her hair in an absent-minded fashion. A slight smile trembled on her mouth, not sure whether this was a friendly encounter or not. Arthur caught her arm, compressing it as if he was making lemonade. With a little manhandling, he navigated her over the elevator's threshold. Before the doors glided shut, he gave Gibson the finger.

"What the hell," Eckhart cried out.

"Don't fret about it. It's not important," Gibson answered even as his insides churned. Arthur's emotional abuse toward Katherine had been cruel and unforgiving. He had cut her off from her friends and family. The bullying had continued unabated until she miscarried. Gibson clutched his fists, wishing he had taken another swing at the bastard.

* * *

They were seated by a young hostess in a cap sleeve blouse and brightly coloured frilly skirt. Tinted windows filtered the sun's intensity, giving the space a warm glow. The panorama view unfolded in high definition. The movement of the revolving dining room was imperceptible. They relaxed in billowy cushions. Gibson glanced two hundred metres below to tiny people snapping selfies and minuscule vehicles roving the streets. He imagined the prime attraction was the renowned Canadian Horseshoe Falls, which spilled tons of water from lake to lake. He never got sick of seeing the fast-flowing river charge past the rocky peak and topple onto the boulders below. Like a train barrelling through the prairie lowlands, there was no speed limit. The mist created by the force sprayed loftier than the steep dive of the water had. Although Gibson couldn't hear the roar from the top of the tower, he knew it was deafening.

Contentment—a feeling of connection to life—overwhelmed him. Something he had misplaced over the last few months. He rolled his neck back and forth and savoured the moment. Bodies of water always brought him peace.

They ordered lunch from an equally young waitress with the same cap sleeve blouse and a vividly coloured skirt. Eckhart twirled her glass of water making the ice cubes clink, breaking the stillness.

"So, what do you think?" Gibson asked as he watched the falls tumble on a never-ending journey.

"About what?" She inclined her head toward her shoulder and peeked sideways.

Gibson discounted her blatantly coquettish manner.

"Elsie." He gazed at the falls when it rotated back into view. "Did the gossiping get her killed in some way? Did she confront someone weeks before? Maybe months ago."

"And what? The killer waited?" Eckhart asked.

"Perhaps. For the perfect stage."

"What could she have said that would make a person go to such extremes?" Eckhart waggled her head in incredulity.

"Maybe she found out someone's nasty secret. Or heaven forbid." The notion smacked him in the face. "Was she blackmailing someone?"

"For what?"

Gibson's weak smile stretched his lip down over his teeth. He was considering the madness of the human race—greed, wealth, power.

"So, whose ring is it?" Eckhart demanded. "Was that a fluke? Was it lost some other time?"

"I'm not sure. We may never break the case. Be prepared for that. You appreciate how it is. We have one print, a partial at that. No match. No straight path to follow."

"I know. Shit. My first case of the Task Force," Eckhart replied. She tugged at the barrette holding her hair into a bun. Her long locks gushed over her shoulders in a free fall. As the view rotated to the west, the late afternoon light slanted through the window and advanced across the tables. It lit her amber hair into a sheaf of gold.

"It happens." Gibson reached over and laid his palm over hers to reassure. No electricity. No jolt. Eckhart jerked her hand back and broke her gaze. A sour and vile taste slipped into Gibson's mouth. He craved to spew the shame away, but realized he had to accept it. He lowered his head and caressed his temple. All he sought was to hear Katherine's gentle voice, her innocence. Was he as rotten as Arthur was? He gritted his teeth until his jaw ached. He thought about the brunette in the pub the other day—Cecilia Sinclair. It was his little fling with her that had ended his first marriage. He had debated, at the time, whether to confess to his wife. Women say they want to know, and then when you tell them they go berserk. But he didn't get a chance to tell her because Cecilia had phoned the house. She had something to tell him. After all these years, he knew what it was. Cecilia had been pregnant with his child. Just like his good buddy had told him. Should he tell Katherine what he had done here? Would she give him a second chance or throw him out of the house? Yeah, he was a rogue.

"Good lunch." His tone dispassionate.

"We should fly. I'll just pop into the ladies' room." Eckhart examined her manicured nails and flipped him a droll smirk. Gibson rose promptly and drew out her chair. He headed for the cashier and settled the bill, ready to get moving. She returned, swinging her handbag as she walked through the din, making heads turn at her beauty. They rode the crowded elevator down in silence, their hands converging briefly. He pressed into the wall. The pavement was hot enough to fry just about anything. His skin glistened with the insufferable temperature, every piece of his clothing getting damp instantly. Eckhart seemed unaffected. A spray from the falls cooled him as he hustled to the truck.

"What next?" She fired up the engine and set the air conditioning to full blast.

"Well." He glanced at his watch. "It's early, but—"

"Are you leaving tomorrow?"

"No. Red-eye Sunday."

"Oh."

"We should have a final run to Lawsons Lane in the morning," Gibson said. Was the answer there? He had a suspicion it was somehow. He had had that feeling all along. If he could only find it. "Last chance for me to look around."

"Okay. I guess it can't hurt," Eckhart replied. She felt they had exhausted all leads, and her case was sunk.

The ride to town was brisk, the growl of the engine pumping out five hundred horsepower with efficiency. Gibson viewed the scenery passing by, not altering much. A long black road rolled out in front, waves of roasted air distorting the perspective. The Expedition didn't falter when they reached the gradient of the high-level bridge—the Garden City Skyway. Six lanes of traffic zoomed over the canal. Gibson glanced in both directions. The waterway stretched for miles. He settled into the leather seat and thought of his family.

* * *

The concrete and wood building accented with a stone facade stood ominously in the offensively bright and cheery sunlight. Jackie and Savannah linked arms as they mounted the steps toward a massive oak door. The wrought iron handle and strapping were as dark as their mood. Savannah leaned into her friend, body quivering and her legs willing to buckle. They crept down the aisle slowly. The aroma of church myrrh incensed the air, wafting over and through the throng of people sitting in metal folding chairs, all lined up in tight formation. Most of them looked uncomfortable, but was it the hard chairs or the fact that Elsie had been murdered that made their waxy faces dour? Their black attire and stilted whispers filled the capacious room.

A mahogany coffin, front and centre, loomed as a dark mass below a wooden crucifix nailed to the wall. Dramatic tributes of gladioli, lilies, chrysanthemums and carnations fought for territory at the front. The abundance of flowers should have been a comfort to Todd, knowing that his wife was well-loved, but he didn't notice anything except the narrow box cloaked in dusty pink roses. He sat in the front row, his gaze flitting from the coffin to the scarred floors and back. His shallow breathing rasped at each intake and stuttered at each exhale. Jackie ushered her friend forward, to the section reserved for family and close acquaintances. When they got there, Savannah looked briefly at the still figure in the mahogany box and wilted into the chair next to her brother-in-law.

"Are you okay?" Jackie asked. She struggled not to cough into the quietude of the cathedral as her voice stuck somewhere halfway down her throat.

Savannah answered with a slight nod and a sharp snort of breath. Jackie sat restlessly beside her friend, adjusting the pleats of her skirt and pressing on her thighs with damp palms. Gregory came into the church on his own and sat behind them.

The preacher delivered a Dylan Thomas poem. Motionlessness embraced Elsie's friends. A shaft of sunlight bore through the stained glass from the arched windows above, attempting to dispel the grief. Burning candles set upon gold-threaded silk cloth on the altar flickered in response. But it was darkness that held the mourners. The preacher's remarks shifted into a lullaby finally allowing the throng to relax. The sorrow scattered, leaving behind only affection for the departed. Jackie seized her companion's hand, shedding her warmth onto the frigid fingers. Jackie closed her eyes and envisioned her existence. Sadness washed over her like frothy waves on a storm-battered coast. A sultry breeze fluttered in through the open door, abating the hotness on her face, offering a fragrance of promise. An angelic hymn floated from the wooden beams to conclude the service. Todd shed no tears. He rose and approached the coffin, stroking the smooth wood as if he sensed Elsie's skin beneath his caress. Savannah wept, the lines on her cheeks testimony to her loss. The whoosh of clothing rarely worn and the shuffling of stiff shoes aroused Jackie from her reverie as people got up from their chairs.

The chatter began. The jangle of wine filled glasses and crystal whiskey tumblers announced the real ceremony. The line-up at the bar snaked around the corner and down the hallway. Men loosened ties that smothered their moist necks, and women pulled at cotton fabric adhering to their sticky legs. Children ran outside and played.

Jackie remained next to Savannah while a chain of condolences bombarded her friend's already faltering resolve. Gregory stood close by, to be there for her but not to impede. The loud exhalation of breath and an occasional moan from Todd was noticed by most. A cursory glance toward Todd confirmed his despair was increasing. A vibration in Jackie's handbag caught her attention. The pulsations throbbed in her palm as she retrieved her cell. She glanced at the text from her mother. 'Dad is home'. Things were moving in a desirable direction. Reggie came over and stood beside Gregory—more support. Not a bead of perspiration spoiled his smooth and dry skin. His suit had a sheen of expensive, a red pinstripe subtly cutting through the black. Jackie smiled and strode outside. She had the airline website in her favourites and booked a flight for that night. Then she called her mom who answered after several rings.

"Sorry, dear. Just getting dad settled." Her tone sounded lighter, freer.

"Dad will be okay now, right?" Jackie asked.

"Yes. The procedure worked. He'll be fine," she answered.

"Mom. That's a relief."

"Yes, it is. How was the funeral? I didn't want to miss it, but I…"

"It was good," Jackie said. "But I'm flying home tonight. I have my own family to take care of. After what Savannah and Todd are going through, I feel like I shouldn't waste a moment. I love you guys."

"I know you do. We love you too," her mom replied.

"I'm on my way now. I'll be there shortly."

"Okay, dear."

Jackie pushed the hang-up button with purpose before she glanced up.

"You're leaving?"

"Yes."

"Take care." Reggie locked onto her emerald eyes and sighed. The one that got away.

Jackie skipped into the hubbub and dragged Savannah into a corner.

"I'm going home now."

"To Victoria?"

"Yes."

The friends hugged, hanging on for several minutes. Jackie climbed into the Lincoln and with a squeal of tires left the parking lot to her parents' house. She rushed inside to see her dad nestled in his favourite spot, a glass clutched in his hand. Jackie froze. Dad chuckled.

"It's tomato juice, honey," he said.

"You bum." Her laughter was a gurgling stream.

"How are you getting to the airport?" her mom shouted down the stairs.

"Shuttle bus."

Soon after, Jackie was leaning back in her seat, headed to the airport. She texted David.

"On my way home. Love you."

Two seconds later, her cell vibrated.

"Same."

* * *

Gibson remained on the balcony watching the last rays of the day slip below the skyline and the shadows steal the night. Dusk brought a refreshing coolness. He looked at the screen on his cell for the hundredth time. No reply. All his calls home had gone to voicemail.

Gibson dropped onto the bed, sinking into its promise of slumber. He was overwrought by the weight of his behaviour. Memories flooded his psyche as his heart thumped with a yearning. He brushed his fingers along the edges of the duvet. The pillow captured his throbbing head. He lay unmoving and caved in to the invitation. After only a couple of fitful hours, he was awakened by a horn honking in the distance and the slamming of a door. The time trickled by, his mind a whirlwind of relentless images until he tumbled back to his nightmare.

Chapter 18

He's racing for the bus and topples; a wisp of black smoke smothers his face. Someone is shaking him.

The shuddering of his cell still clasped in his fist awakened him. Startled, Gibson sat up promptly, slinging out his arm. The phone eluded his grasp and thudded along the floor in a spiral. He heard a bang as it deflected off some object, maybe the desk. Gibson vaulted off the bed, presuming it had come to rest somewhere between the bathroom and an armchair. His foot caught the edge and kicked it across the suite toward the glass door. He just about knocked the lamp off the bedside table fumbling with the switch. Finally, he snatched it and answered, "Gibson," uncertain who was on the other end; not confident it was even functioning after its gymnastic workout.

"Honey. Is that you?"

Light surged into the room.

"Katherine. Where have you been?"

"Oh, silly. Didn't you get my text?"

Gibson gawked at the symbol on the shattered screen indicating incoming text. "I guess I must have fallen asleep. Miss you."

"I miss you, too," Katherine replied. "I have some bad news."

Gibson sucked in his breath.

"And a marvelous announcement."

"Okay." His heart stopped and restarted.

"The awful news is that I had my fingerprints taken."

"What?" It skittered another beat.

"For my new position," Katherine squealed, oblivious to her husband's heartbeat. "At a bank. Actually, several branches. As a relief assistant manager—"

"That's the bad story?"

"Don't fret, my prints won't be run. They're put on file for reference. Not that it matters. I haven't killed anyone lately." She giggled.

Gibson thought life was so bizarre.

"Do you require the good news?"

"Yes." Gibson detected a note of enormity in her tone. The twitter of her zebra finches played in the background.

"We're going to have a baby," Katherine said. After a protracted hesitation, she asked, "Are you still there?"

"Oh, my god," Gibson answered. Blinking lashes heavy with dampness unleashed. Tears rolled from his smoky eyes, down his cheeks and stuck onto his trembling chin. A sobbing escaped from his throat and reached down the line to his wife. He fingered the screen. "I love you Katherine. I can hardly wait to see you."

"Me, too. Tomorrow then," Katherine said and hung up.

Gibson's heart crashed into a rib. He held the phone to his chest. There's no place like home. He stepped into the shower and spun the dial to its hottest. He pressed his forehead against the frigid tiles, letting the steamy rivulets trickle down his back. The water ran chilly as he stood in a daze. He let the spray pummel his muscles as his mind whirled and clicked. Craving to get the day done, he dressed hurriedly and left the motel. He skipped down the sidewalk. A sparrow soared by his nose and docked on the same hanging basket as the days before. The peeping of chicks caught his awareness. He watched three tiny mouths stretch high to capture food from mom's beak. Or maybe it was dad? He produced a two-step on the pavement and floated to the café, his loose-fitting shirt already clinging to his back from the heat. Gibson glanced at his watch. It was just seven. The sun would hammer down with unforgiving devilry today. The Expedition came to a halt across the street. He hopped in and sent Eckhart a quirky smile. All was perfect in his world.

She gave him a sidelong glare, her pale lips dipped into a sulky pout. "Lawsons Lane here we come. You never know." She was totally annoyed with the investigation going in circles.

"Work the case until nothing is left behind," he replied.

Gibson leaned back to relish the final ride to the crime scene. He looked out the window as they whizzed by sports fields, two high schools, blocks of houses and apartments. The tires crossed silently over a railway track. As they neared the canal, a sequence of siren blasts sounded.

"Oh, shit," Eckhart said. She slowed and halted in front of the striped barriers that had dropped down to block access to the bridge. Red lights blinked across the hood in a hypnotic cadence. "About an hour," she acknowledged the unasked question.

"I see." A blue labyrinth of metal rose skyward, the counterweight bearing down on them.

"Don't worry, it won't strike us," she said.

The gears wound slowly until the deck stood vertically in the air. A siren blared. The lock swung open wide. The ship passed by, rust stains running down the empty hull standing tall in the water. Gibson wanted to reach out and touch the foreign entity. Another outburst of the signal and the gates locked behind the stern. The bridge made its plunge earthbound, hitting the ground with a thunk that jolted the truck. Whoa.

"Haven't witnessed that in a while," Gibson said.

Eckhart drove faster than usual to make up for the squandered time. As she shifted into the lane, a Range Rover sped toward the beach ahead of them, dust drifting in vast arcs around the vehicle. Gibson squinted after it. Was that Reggie? Eckhart pulled into Jacobs Landing with a crunching of tires and flung the gears into park. "Okay. Made it."

Gibson frowned at the increasing amount of graffiti on the store walls. Across the weathered boards of the porch, someone had callously painted, 'Fattie.' The red lettering stood out on the dark wood. He was perturbed not only at the damage but by the poor taste of words. He stepped out of the vehicle and relished the gentle breeze from the lake. Although it beat the temperature back a few degrees, it wasn't enough to check the sweat rolling down his neck and soaking his collar. They walked along the pathway, sensing the emptiness of the house. He knocked on the door, but there was no answer.

"Should we try Grandma's house?" she asked.

"Yup. We might be offered a frosty drink even if she has nothing more to tell us," Gibson answered as he wiped the glisten from his forehead.

Sparrows, finches and towhees darted across the road as Eckhart crept down Lawsons Lane. Their offbeat clatter warned of further warmth to develop. In the meadow between the two houses, a hawk sat stationary in a towering maple. With a sudden swoop, the raptor plummeted through the pasture and pounced on an unsuspecting prey. He flew back to the tree with a mouse in his large beak. Eckhart steered into Grandma's yard. She was on the veranda relaxing in the shade.

"Wasn't expecting to see you again," Grandma said. She waved a palm to the wicker armchairs. "Looks like you could use a lemonade." She scuttled inside without waiting for a response.

Eckhart slumped onto a bench, stretching her bare legs over the cushion. The rattling of glasses and banging of doors drifted from the kitchen. Grandma pushed on the screen door with her shoulder, her hands engaged with a tray of drinks and biscuits. She deposited it on the side table and plopped back into her rocker. Her skin had a reddish hue from working in the sunlight—a farmer's face marked with sharp creases. She fastened her untamed hair into a messy bun. Her laughter captivated, so generous of personality. Gibson transferred his chair over to Grandma and settled in for a chitchat.

"Gregory is a decent lad," Grandma said out of the blue.

"He's fortunate to have your loyalty," Gibson replied.

"He wanted to be a schoolteacher like his dad."

"Felton was a teacher? I assumed he retired from farming."

"Oh, no. He taught for twenty-five years," she replied. "Gregory planned to follow in his footsteps until the rape thing."

"What grade did Felton teach?"

"College. He adored it. When he first started, they took his fingerprints. Boy, he was livid. He said it made him feel like a common criminal," she answered. Her soft, stooped shoulders jerked with amusement.

"What school was that?" Gibson shifted his chair in tighter and leaned forward.

"Niagara Peninsula."

Gibson pushed back in his seat. What had Katherine said? They would hold her prints on file. He let his mind flit to the probabilities as he quaffed the refreshing drink.

"We should get moving. Thanks for the snacks. Take care," Gibson said as he squeezed Grandma's arm. Her eyes twinkled as if she knew his secret.

They hopped into the truck. Eckhart fired it up and carried out a three-point turn.

"We should find Felton's prints. It's a lead. What do you think?"

"Sure. As you once said, leave no rock unturned."

"I didn't say that."

"Well, it was something like that," she replied.

* * *

Reggie glanced in his rear-view mirror. He was positive that was the Expedition pulling into the store. No matter. He peered at Savannah and gave her a lopsided grin.

"Are you okay?"

"Yes." She grew rigid, the truck bouncing down the lane.

Reggie swung right and lined up next to Gregory's Honda. He vaulted out of the Rover. Savannah remained suspended in her seat. He bent back down at the window and stared at her.

"Aren't you joining me?"

"Felton and Margaret don't like me."

"They will after they find out what I have to say."

Savannah wet her lips and made a jerky bob of acknowledgment. She gripped the handle and thrust the door open after a moment's doubt. Her hand passed along the fender as she rounded the vehicle, booting up dust with her canvas sneakers. Reggie turned and signaled her up the stairs.

"It's all right."

"I'm the man of the house." A deep, gravelly remark overrode the babbling voices.

"Felton. Put that cigarette out," Margaret yelled.

Savannah halted mid-stomp.

"Stop, Mom," Gregory pleaded.

The screen creaked as Felton poked his way outside. He froze at the sight of Savannah, pointing a finger at her. "What the hell is she doing here?"

"Leave her alone," Gregory said. He rushed out and stood beside Savannah, draping his arm over her shoulder and steered her to the swing. The long-rusted chains squeaked as they swung back and forth.

"Take it easy, Felton. I have great news for you guys."

"What?" He hacked, and then spat over the railing.

Savannah flinched.

Margaret wavered in the doorway. Her annoyance plainly displayed in the pinched expression. Her eyebrows formed a continuous row across her forehead. She stepped outside and plunked into her chair, propping her swollen legs on the ottoman.

"What's this all about, Reggie?"

"Yeah. Get on with it." Felton lit up another fag, blasting out the smoke with vigour toward Savannah. He collapsed next to his wife.

"Okay. This isn't definite, but I studied the transcripts from Gregory's trial and discovered an egregious mistake—"

"What?" Margaret shouted.

Reggie held up his palm. "Let me finish. The prosecutor utilized two different shops to analyze DNA from Gregory and the victim." He winked at the lovebirds. "It's probable there was a muddle at the lab."

Gregory grinned. He knew.

"Your son presented me a specimen last week for a retest. I had it run through rapid DNA technology at the Centre of Forensic Sciences."

Margaret squealed.

"The upshot is that the DNA from the rape incident is not Gregory's." Reggie stayed his palm repeatedly. "Settle down. They don't recognize rapid DNA results in the courts. However, we further dispatched a sample for routine inspection through the RCMP laboratory. That requires at least forty days." He flapped his hand back and forth to stop Margaret from interrupting. "But we're confident when we receive those, they will establish Gregory's innocence."

Felton sputtered again. The gob missed the rail and landed on the deck. Savannah scrunched her nose.

"We'll sue the bastards," Margaret declared. An arrogant laugh spewed from her greasy lips.

"Forget it, Mom. I'm thrilled just to be exonerated," Gregory said. He dropped his chin to his chest and bawled. "All those years lost."

Savannah planted a palm over her mouth, a single tear eased down her cheek.

Chapter 19

"What the hell?" Eckhart slammed on her brakes inches from the bumper of the Ford F1. The burgundy pickup had cut the corner sharply into the one lane driveway.

"That's Anatoe. Let's see where he's been." Gibson hopped out of the Expedition and strolled over to the old truck. Eckhart sauntered up from behind and propped her elbows on the hood.

"Hey, do you mind?" Anatoe yelled.

"Sorry." Eckhart jumped away from the truck, holding her hands up.

"What now?" Anatoe rested into his seat and scowled at Gibson.

"Where's the Chevy?" Gibson looked into the brown eyes, hoping they would be as soulful as his mom's one day.

"I sold it."

"Where've you been?"

"In Grimsby. A guy there bought it."

"I see. Took you two days?"

"What's it to you? Am I under arrest?"

"Not at all," Gibson replied.

"Hey, look. I didn't kill Elsie," he said. "I had a few days off and hung out with my buddies. That's all. Even Todd got time off."

"What's that?" Gibson asked and leaned on the window frame.

"I saw Todd at a coffee shop—"

"In Grimsby?" Gibson interrupted.

"Yeah."

"Who was he with?"

"Josephine," Anatoe replied, pressing his thin lips into a line, not wanting to be the snitch.

"Okay." Gibson drummed twice on the door with his palm and pushed off. He swung toward the house and saw Grandma staring in their direction. Was that a warning to keep his secret to himself? Gibson hesitated. Should he tell Anatoe the truth? That he was Anatoe's father. No. He had no right to interfere with the guy's life.

"Take care, Anatoe. Say hi to your mom."

He hopped into the Expedition with Eckhart following suit. Anatoe guided his pickup past their vehicle and remained at the entrance, watching as they veered into the street and out of sight. Gibson thought maybe Cecilia might tell Anatoe if he asked her the right question.

"Todd is implicated in something. Isn't he?"

"We need to bring him in for questioning to get to the bottom of this," Gibson said.

"So it wasn't a one-night stand. He's having an affair. And maybe wanted it to be more? Get rid of the wife?" Eckhart asked.

"It's definitely a strong possibility," he replied.

"Do you think Elsie knew about the affair and was threatening him?"

"We don't know anything at this point. Let's start by finding Todd and getting him to the station downtown."

"Okay." Eckhart turned to him and almost whacked the guardrail at Jacobs Landing. They hurried down the path for the second time that day, but nobody answered the door.

"Maybe he's still in Grimsby. And where is Savannah?" Gibson asked. He pulled out his cell and dialed the DC.

"Cooper. I want surveillance at Todd's place. And bring Jones with you. Stay there until he shows up. I don't care if it takes all day and all night. Just make sure you bring him in. He's not under arrest, but he is under suspicion for murdering his wife. I need answers," Gibson said. He hung up and crammed the phone into his back pocket.

"Whoa. Really. You're really thinking it could be Todd?"

Gibson shrugged.

"What did Cooper say to that?"

"He was surprised, but will get on it."

"I bet."

"Today's Saturday. Will the college be open?"

"It's always open," Eckhart replied.

"Let's go."

"But, I thought—"

"We don't know anything for certain. Follow all the leads," Gibson reiterated.

"Right." Eckhart thrust the gears into reverse and backed out. At the stop sign, she took a left and sped down Lakeshore Road, past several wineries and fruit stands. Just after the cemetery, she turned and followed the street, swerving with the dogleg. Gibson stared out the window to the vast orchards eating up the land. The college loomed ahead, all glass and metal—that seemed to be a theme in this town. A remorseless sun gleamed off the mirrored panels, exacerbating the already fiery rays. The parking lot was packed so she bounced over the curb at the front of the building and stopped.

"That'll do," Eckhart said.

Stone stairs swept steeply up. Students loitered on their coolness with their backpacks sprawling every which way.

There was plenty of laughter and kissing in the corners. The ornate doors opened smoothly with a steady surge of bodies in and out. Inside the grand entrance, a black arrow clearly marked the path to the office. The receptionist was a middle-aged woman with mousy brown hair swept up with rhinestone clasps. A colourful scarf covered the wrinkles forming on her neck.

Gibson leaned on the counter, provided a lopsided smile and took out his badge. Eckhart flashed her ID as well.

"Officers. How may I serve you?" she asked. Her grin was practiced, but nevertheless sincere.

"We're interested in reviewing a teacher's file. A retired teacher," Gibson said.

"You have a warrant?" She looked at him over her black-rimmed glasses. Her smile intensified, pushing creases from the edge of her lips. Gibson screwed up his face.

"I didn't think so," she said and rapped her fingers on the laminate top. "Who are we talking about?"

"Felton Cunningham."

"I see." The thrumming continued. "I'll make an exception. Follow me."

Gibson swung the flimsy gate. It struck the side of the counter with a wallop.

"Sorry. Didn't realize my strength."

"Don't worry. That's not the first time that has happened. It needs to be adjusted," she replied.

The inner sanctuary was a maze of corridors. After turning several corners, the receptionist halted in front of a paneled door with brass fittings. She sifted through a jumble of keys and unlocked the storage room. The space was larger than he thought it would be. It was more of a study room. A long table monopolized the area, its luminous polish showing off the whorls of the wood. Six chairs shoved in the corner looked antique.

"Have a seat. This will barely take me a moment."

Gibson and Eckhart pulled up chairs and sat. The receptionist opened several drawers before locating the correct carton. "We're scanning everything into digital files. But we haven't made it to the 'Cs' yet. It's a slow process." She dumped the binder on the tabletop. "If you need his spouse's register, we'll have to move to the dungeon. It was so long ago."

"Pardon me." Gibson's chin shot up. "Margaret?"

"Yes. His wife was a substitute teacher way back when. That's how they met. She gave up the job when they got married."

"I see," Gibson said.

"Do you need it?" she asked.

"I suppose we do." Gibson locked eyes with Eckhart.

"Well, have a gander at that. I won't be long." She jiggled the keys. "Have to pick up the ancient ones." She sauntered out the room laughing, a delightful chuckle.

The detectives pushed their chairs close together, knees touching, and huddled over the file. Gibson picked up a cardboard jacket marked prints.

"Really. That simple." He opened the package gingerly and drew out the card with Felton's imprint. It was a perfect print and hadn't smudged over the years.

"Awesome."

Gibson put the card back in the envelope and set it aside. He flipped the pages carefully, tracing down the edges with his fingertip. A criminal records check was on the top. There were plenty of performance reports and wage hikes. Then a discipline letter got his attention. He thumbed through it.

"It's an incident with a pupil. Fifteen years ago. It's very vague about what happened, and there was no action taken against Felton," he said.

He skimmed through a dozen more evaluations. There was nothing striking, nothing that caught his eye until he turned to the final sheet in the folder.

"What have we here?" Gibson asked. He knocked his knuckles on the table.

"They fired Felton," Eckhart said as she peered at the letter.

"Yes, so it seems."

"Sexual misconduct. They granted him a pass the first time."

"Not as tolerable in the 'Me-too' environment," Gibson replied.

The door handle jangled, and the receptionist breezed into the chamber, her flowered skirt flowing behind. "Got what you were searching for?" She smirked.

"Why are Felton's prints here?" Gibson asked.

"Let me clarify why we have his prints. We have every teacher's prints. Actually, every applicant. The Criminal Records Review Agency does a records check on everyone that applies for a job with the school board. And not only teachers but all staff. They take the prints but only run them through the RCMP data if something relevant shows up during their enquiries. Something like a DUI. Felton's prints are still here because he had no kind of unlawful history and nothing came up while he was on staff. It's as simple as that. We continue to conduct criminal checks this way to be fair to both the staff and the students. Rarely does an unsavoury person get by us."

"Can we keep the prints?"

"What prints?" the receptionist asked.

Gibson realized she didn't like Felton but didn't want to get herself into trouble either. That was cool with him.

The dungeon was a floor below, a windowless basement. It didn't smell musky but was cool and well lit. The receptionist trotted at a brisk pace, her crepe soles making a soft squelching noise. They clip-clopped after her down the narrow corridor, single file like children do. She halted in front of a grey steel door, her shoes squeaking from the abrupt motion.

"Let me figure out what room it is. Haven't been here in a while." She referred to a note in an alloy frame beside the entryway. "Nope, not this one." She proceeded along and considered two more placards before announcing, "Here we are."

When she opened the door, a light turned on immediately. It was a limited space comparable to a storage locker. Boxes piled to the ceiling leaned precariously on the right side. She shrugged her shoulders. "I'll leave you to it. Come visit me before you take off." She spun around and asked, "Will you find your way out?"

"I expect so. I left behind a trail of breadcrumbs," Gibson said.

The receptionist grinned, her lips lifting upwards. The beam reached her eyes. "Good luck." She thought of something else and pivoted toward them. "Margaret's maiden name is Sayward."

She retreated down the hallway, the squelching sound providing her whereabouts.

"Nice lady."

"Yeah. Where do we start?" Eckhart asked.

Gibson tugged at his collar and gaped at the containers. They were labelled, but the years had faded the ink. He passed his palm along the stickers, pressing them back in place as he worked. They hauled down boxes and examined their contents. The search went on for ages as they dismissed irrelevant files. Finally, Eckhart yanked out a binder with 'Margaret Sayward' faintly imprinted in blue.

"Got it," she said. Her hands shook as she flipped it open. There were two formal letters and a brown envelope. "Her resume and acceptance letter. And behind door number three." She tipped the sleeve and a print card dropped into her palm. "Ta-da!"

"All right. We're set," Gibson said and tucked the treasure into his front pocket with Felton's.

"But Felton is lame and Margaret is fat. Pardon my politically incorrect terminology," Eckhart said.

"That's true, but at least we have two prints to run we didn't have a few hours ago. You never know," Gibson said. He agreed with Eckhart and didn't expect the prints to bring them any closer to a murderer, but it chased the day away. One more night and a morning.

Eckhart curled her pale pink lips and rolled her eyes. They clambered up the concrete steps. At the halfway point, Gibson's cell chirped. He looked at the text.

"They picked up Todd. I guess there isn't any mobile coverage in the basement. They got him an hour ago."

"Okay, that's something," Eckhart said. They were going in so many directions, it was making her brain spin. She just wanted something to pan out. They climbed the rest of the stairs and found their way back to the front desk without any problems.

"Thanks for everything," Gibson said.

The receptionist offered a shrewd grin and retired to her keyboard. The clacking of keys was fast and steady.

The heat struck like a tsunami wave as Gibson opened the main door outside.

"Holy shit. It's sizzling out here," Eckhart said. The Expedition sat where she had left it hopped up on the curb. The waves of heat off the hood were visible even from the top of the steps. They held the truck doors open for a few minutes to let the hot air escape. It fired up admirably, and soon frosty air flowed out the vents. Eckhart slapped the dashboard. "Good truck."

Gibson sat back and depressed the lever at the side of his seat, allowing himself a few more inches of space. His spine felt compressed by the session of tugging heavy boxes off towering ledges.

"Let's shoot the prints over to the station first."

"Okay."

Gibson plucked his cell out. He had it in a front pocket this time. The call dispatched to voicemail after ten rings. "Damn. Frenchy isn't there." He glimpsed at his wristwatch. "Oh, it's six already. Guess someone has a life."

"Not us," Eckhart said.

He dialed another number. When Cooper finally answered, Gibson spoke for several minutes before disconnecting the call.

"What's going on with Frenchy?" Eckhart asked after he hung up.

"She went to a concert in Toronto with Reggie."

"Really? What did Cooper say about the prints we found?"

"Not a lot. He was surprised. Hey, we missed lunch today and I'm ravenous. What about you?" On cue his belly rumbled.

"Sure. Where to?"

"The Mansion House. It's near the police station. We can nip in there afterward."

"That'll work," she said. "Should we give Rodney a heads up as well?"

"I'll shoot him a text. Undoubtedly he's left the office."

"Yeah."

* * *

It was seven by the time they dropped off the prints and headed back to town. It was Saturday night, and the streets were crawling with people dining out and pub hopping. The lone theatre had a queue that vanished around the corner. There wasn't one spot to park either so Eckhart hit the police lot.

"Should we go in first?" Gibson asked. His stomach growled in revolt with no means to muzzle the noise except to feed the beast. "Forget it. Let's dine."

Even as the sun dipped lower in the sky, the intensity of the day ebbed slowly. They zipped down the sizzling pavement to the pub. A live band pumped rock 'n' roll, country style, into the street. They grabbed one of the last free tables, happy to sit still at last. It looked as if the waiter was overworked so they sat back and enjoyed the music while they waited. Their server finally came over, and Eckhart ordered a wine while Gibson asked for the on-tap house beer. The burgers would get there when they got there. What can you do? Gibson checked the screen when his cell chirped. It was the superintendent.

'Excellent job, you guys. Call me in the morning.'

Eckhart leaned in so she could read the message.

"Cool."

Their food made it before long, and they ate in silence, enjoying the band. Gibson drummed on his thighs to the rhythm. At the windup of the first set, they headed outside to a cooler night air. The sun's stifling rays had perished behind the escarpment in the west. They walked back to the station to see about a visit. Gibson rang the bell and held up his badge to the camera as he spoke to the dispatcher.

"We would like to visit Todd Webber."

"No can do," the officer responded.

"Okay. Why's that?"

"Lights out at 2100."

Gibson glanced at his watch. The glare of the spotlights directed at the entrance made it challenging to see the glowing digits.

"Right. In the morning then. Thanks." He swung to Eckhart. "A hell of a day. Drop me off?"

"Sure."

Gibson rolled down his window and let the coolness flood his fevered skin. He gazed up at the sky and saw a shooting star zip through the constellation Sagittarius. It hung low near the southern horizon with the Milky Way spread as an immense ribbon of luminosity in the background. He wondered if Katherine had seen the flash.

"There you go," Eckhart said as she pulled up to his motel.

Gibson skipped down the passage to his suite. He flopped into an armchair and tossed his cell on the duvet.

His hair was slick, and his face had a glossy sheen from the day-long oppressive heat. He wanted another shower to cool his thoughts. Thousands of droplets bombarded his skin as he stood under the refreshing water. The sensation consoled his mind as a weariness overcame his body. He collapsed into bed, tired as hell. A soft snore flooded the room as he let go of the day. Even the phone pressing into his ribs when he rolled over didn't disturb his rest.

Chapter 20

Nighttime surrendered to the dawn. The soft light snuck through curtains left partially open, slanting onto the bed sheets and licked Gibson's sunburnt face. He was buried in sleep. The sun broke clear of its boundary, and the rays tumbled into the suite. He drifted into consciousness and smoothed his tired eyes. He squeezed his cheek to the flattened pillow.

His cell chirped. 'Soon. Katherine.' He drew in a breath and texted back. 'Not soon enough.'

Gibson showered again and put on the last clean shirt he had and his wedding band. Packing his bag took two seconds and he was out the exit. The fresh morning air was still. There would be no cooling breeze to break the sweltering fever that the amber sun promised for the day. He looked for the sparrow as he strolled down the sidewalk. The bird flirted with his hair as she bustled past. Gibson chuckled and continued to the café. He grabbed a coffee and waited on the patio for his ride. The Expedition stuck its snout into the street fifteen minutes later. He hopped in and threw Eckhart a quirky smile.

"Is Frenchy in the office?"

"Not yet." She stared at his hand.

"Should we go visit Todd first?" Gibson asked.

"You bet," Eckhart replied. She sped downtown in record time and parked in the same spot as the night before, twirling the keys in her fingers.

"We should run Todd's prints first. Do you concur?"

"I do."

The desk sergeant directed them to an area at the rear of the building. "His lawyer's here."

Loud voices stole down the corridor. They followed the sound to an interview room on the left where a frenzied conversation was going on.

"Hello." Gibson knocked on the door, and it swung open with a squeak.

"This is a confidential conversation."

"No. Let them in. I want to know what's going on," Todd said and jumped out of his chair.

"Don't say anything," a small man with neat hair said.

"To hell with that. I didn't kill my wife. Why would I?" Todd's shrill voice ricocheted off the lead-coloured surfaces. He slumped back into his chair. A scuffle exploded into the room.

"What's happening here?" Savannah demanded as she ran to her brother-in-law.

"Sorry, sir. I couldn't stop her," an officer said as he rushed up behind the frantic woman.

"It's okay. Let her be," Gibson replied.

The officer shuffled back to his duties at the front.

"Everybody have a seat. Let's get this straightened out." Gibson's cell vibrated in his back pocket. "Excuse me a moment." He stepped into the hallway. The scrape of metal legs on linoleum followed him out as everyone settled in.

"Gibson."

"It's Frenchy. I received your message. I'm at the office."

"That's great. Could you do Todd's prints first? We'll be standing by," he said. "Thanks for coming in on such short notice."

"No problem."

Gibson disconnected and entered the stuffy box. His forehead took on a glossy shine almost at once. He scanned the faces at the table. Todd sagged heavily in a chair between his lawyer and Savannah. He looked a mess, but it was his raspy breathing that unsettled Gibson. His lawyer sat up straight with a briefcase and a straw hat by his hand. He shuffled the paperwork that he had laid before him on the tabletop. A fine tailored suit of grey matched his eyes, a lustrous patina of burnished metal. But the neon red in his striped tie clocked him a rebel. He tapped his polished black loafers on the crumbling tiles impatiently. Savannah sat on the brink of her seat, knotting her fists under her knees to control the desire to strike out at the enemy. The scowl on her pink mouth made her look ten years older. Eckhart sat quietly, but the glint in her blue eyes exposed her mischievous spirit.

Gibson selected a seat by the recording equipment and considered his options.

"Let's do this off the record," he finally said. He looked up to the top corner of the room and made sure the red button on the camera wasn't on.

"Off the record? Seriously," Eckhart retorted.

Gibson glanced at her as she opened her mouth and hissed in dispute. Her pink lips paled as she nibbled on a pencil. He arched his steel-grey eyes and locked onto her indignation. She flipped her hair and strummed her nails on the blemished wood. Todd leaned forward, but his lawyer seized his arm attempting to block his progress. He sought to tear away.

"Be quiet," his lawyer said and tightened his constraint.

Gibson's cell chirped, and he glimpsed at the screen.

"It'll be all right. Let him talk," the detective said, throwing a nod of promise to the lawyer.

There was a wild look about Todd. His slept-in clothing shouted a stench from the gutters. The pallor of his skin looked worse than the last corpse he had seen. Gibson clenched his teeth, thinking the last corpse he had seen was Elsie.

"Why did you meet up with Josephine? Are you having an affair?" Gibson asked calmly, his pit-bull having a nap.

"No. Nothing like that." His lips smacked when he spoke. He planted his elbows on the table and pressed his fingers on his forehead. Beads of perspiration dribbled down his temples, reeking of fret. "I couldn't stand it any further."

"Stand what?"

The lawyer touched his client's shoulder.

"JoJo wouldn't stop phoning. I told her it had been a mistake. I told you that earlier," Todd said. Even his swollen eyes were pale.

Gibson waited to hear more and Todd obliged.

"I went there to make it perfectly clear to her that nothing was going on. To leave me alone. I love Elsie." The sweat flowed liberally and intermingled with his tears. His body heaved with anguish, with a heartache that would never leave.

Gibson almost felt sorry for the man, knowing that he had not been the perfect husband either. It wasn't his job to judge.

"We ran your prints already. They're not yours. You're free to go," Gibson said, catching everyone off guard.

Savannah let out a wail and swept Todd into a hug. Eckhart walked out of the room. In a snit? Gibson wasn't certain.

"Sorry," Gibson said.

"I'm glad we've cleared that up. Thank you," Todd's lawyer replied.

The gentleman shook hands. Gibson left them to their sorrow.

Eckhart was already out the station. He jogged after her. "Hang on." She scorned him. "What's wrong?" he called out. She banged the truck door and fired up the motor. He hopped into the passenger side.

"That's it."

"What?"

"We've run out of suspects." She glowered at him, awaiting the rebuke.

"Sometimes—"

"Yeah, I realize sometimes the case goes unsolved." She mimicked him with a growl deep in her throat.

His cell sounded again. 'Not Felton.'

Eckhart snatched his phone and glared at the screen. "Right." She tossed it into his lap and reeled out of the parking lot. The Expedition rumbled down the street, taking corners with considerable velocity. Gibson pushed into his seat and kept his eyes and mouth sealed. She squealed the tires onto the tarmac and slapped the gear into park. He remained inert, waiting for the storm to ease. She glimpsed at him.

"Sorry. I'm so frustrated with this case," Eckhart said. "How ungrateful of me after all your help."

"I get it. We have one last shot. Then, we'll write up a report," he replied.

"Okay." Her whisper tinged with humiliation.

Gibson barely noticed the heat as he headed to the building.

"When's your flight?" Eckhart asked, the ruffles calmed. She strolled beside him and unlocked the door with her key card.

"The red-eye at midnight. Lots of time yet." He gave a tiny quirk of a smile.

"It won't be long. I put Margaret's prints in already." Frenchy stood in front of the computer, waiting for the results to appear. The three of them took vigilance, holding their breath. The hard drive whirled. The monitor went dark. It lit up. A positive match.

"What the hell!" Eckhart shrieked. "Are you kidding me?" She grabbed Gibson's arm and jumped up and down. "Oh, my god. This is incredible." She broke off and studied Frenchy. "Is this a false reading? A joke?"

"No." The lab technician shook her head, utterly bewildered herself.

Gibson couldn't express his bemusement.

"But why? That's crazy."

"Let's go get her," Gibson said.

Eckhart babbled as she raced to the truck. She chattered all the way down Lakeshore Drive, over the canal and to Jacobs Landing. A long string of vehicles rocketed down the road from Niagara-on-the-Lake. At the first opportunity in traffic, she zoomed across the yellow line to Lawsons Lane. Gibson glanced at the store as they flew by. It seemed desolate, devoid of soul. Eckhart continued down the lane, dust spilling out in the aftermath of the tires, choking off vision behind them. Flocks of sparrows fled from the shrubs on the roadway, dodging the mayhem. She slowed down and sneaked up behind Felton's vehicle. Gregory's motorbike parked on the grass had fallen on its side. Before Gibson got out, he patted her hand. She looked over. Her eyes had changed to an icy blue.

"It's your play."

Eckhart nodded and hopped out of the truck. Gibson followed her to the steps, waiting on the bottom tread. Felton sat on the swing, blowing smoke through his nose.

"What now?" He coughed twice, and then took another drag on his cigarette. "Margaret, you've got company," he yelled. Felton hacked again, making fat tears roll down his face.

"For Christ sakes, Felton. Spit it out," Margaret rebuked.

He shot a giant gob of phlegm toward the garden. It missed its mark and landed on the deck.

"Jesus. Just more work for me," Margaret grumbled. She stalked to the kitchen and came back with a mop, slamming the door behind her. "Disgusting. It's like cleaning the bathroom after you." She brushed at the wood with little progress. "Damn." She flung the mop against the railing and plunked into the floral cushions.

Eckhart waited for her opportunity to speak.

"Margaret Cunningham you are—"

"What am I?"

"You're under arrest for the murder of Elsie Webber," Eckhart said and stepped forward. "Stand up." Her voice thundered with authority. Gibson lifted his eyebrows at the force of her assertion.

"Felton." Margaret pressed into her chair.

"What?" He spat out another hunk.

"Get up." Eckhart took one further stride forward.

"This is ridiculous. Felton, call our lawyer," Margaret demanded. She rose, dragging her hands along her skirt to flatten the creases.

"Yeah, I will," he said but remained seated as Eckhart clamped on the handcuffs and led Margaret to the Expedition. Gibson opened the rear door and eased her inside.

"Go away." Margaret jerked his hand off. She sat up straight, a grandiose pinch to her mouth and dead eyes fixed forward.

Felton ground his smoke on the deck and lit another one as they pulled out of the driveway. Every once in a while, Margaret protested her predicament, but they couldn't make out her words through the thick glass partition that divided the front and back space. When they reached the intersection, Gibson looked over to Jacobs Landing. There was a flurry of activity on the veranda. Gregory and Savannah were scrubbing vigorously at the windows to remove the filth, a soapy bucket of water between them. Their laughter streamed out and travelled down to the beach and across the lake. Gregory didn't notice his mother in the police vehicle, having eyes only for Savannah.

Eckhart reached for the switches on the dashboard. She glanced toward Gibson before flipping them on. His quirky smile gave the okay. The drive to the downtown station was speedy with the accompaniment of the siren and lights. She had phoned ahead to give instructions. Two officers waited at the entrance for the Expedition to arrive. Without any fuss, Margaret was taken into custody, the steel door clanging behind her ample body.

Chapter 21

Gibson phoned Cooper and told him the news. "Go visit your favourite judge. Get a warrant for Felton's place. Everything. Not just the house." He assigned a few more directives and signed off.

"Lunch while we wait?" Eckhart asked.

"Perfect."

They ambled down Church Street to the pub. A fresh breeze had sprung up and blew gusts of cool respite. They settled into their preferred spot and ordered. It wasn't hectic so the refreshments came right away. Gibson chugged his beer, wiping the foam off his lips.

"I was parched," he said. "You did fine."

"It's hard to believe. What the hell happened between Margaret and Elsie?" Eckhart asked.

"I don't know, but we'll unearth the truth." He pressed to his temple. An image had come and gone.

They chatted while they dined. Gibson sat back in his chair and polished off his drink.

"We should mosey on. Ready?"

"Yup."

Gibson settled the bill, and they walked down the shady side of the street to the station. Margaret's lawyer hadn't arrived yet so Gibson rested on the bench in the foyer. He leaned against the hard wall painted a nondescript green, like slime, and passed the time with a game of solitaire on his cell. Eckhart leaned against the wall, too anxious to sit still.

"How much does Felton know about all this? We should pull him in for a chat," Gibson said, looking up at his partner.

"You're right."

Gibson punched the redial button. "Cooper. Could you bring Felton in? He's not under arrest." He hung up. "On the way."

Sultry air slinked in when the main door opened. A man dressed in a brown suit and elegant brown shoes stepped inside. His bushy brows bent over droopy eyelids like a basset hound, and his beaky nose was drippy. Fat lips bunched into a harsh frown down to his double chin. His teeth moved as if he was chewing cud. He peered at Gibson as he tottered to the counter. With a loud harrumph, he cleared his throat and said, "I'm Philip Smith, Margaret Cunningham's attorney. Where is she?"

Gibson glanced up. The man clung with wrinkled hands to a briefcase that looked traumatized from years of scraping under courtroom benches. The officer at the desk led the way down the corridor. The elderly man moved unsteadily after him, his hard-soled wingtips making a disturbing clack on the linoleum. Gibson tossed his chin toward Eckhart. She stealthily shadowed the two figures to Margaret's lockup. A metal chair just outside the door shouted her name. She sat down on the cold surface prepared to wait it out for the long haul. The officer pitched her a grin and headed back to his post. The lawyer snarled, a short fizz escaping his parted lips.

Another sweltering rush of air whistled in. Two constables stepped into the station and crossed the lobby with their quarry sardined between them. Cooper turned and winked, hoisting his chin with a sniff. Jones took a wide stance at the counter and anchored his free hand on his hip. Felton gawked at Gibson with an outraged frown, his forehead furrowing into cavernous creases. After the constables clocked in their detainee, Gibson rose to accompany the parade down the corridor. He seized the steel handle of an interview room and yanked on the weighty door.

They all piled inside the tiny square room painted a shiny gunmetal grey, designed to instill apprehension. The fluorescent lights flickered and buzzed when Gibson flipped the switch revealing four orange plastic chairs and a plywood table. Gibson gestured to the far side of the narrow table. Felton sat and placed his fists on his knees. His shoulders took on the configuration of the non-ergonomic chair, forcing his shoulders to sag forward. He looked ghostly in the bold light.

"Thanks guys. I'll take it from here," Gibson said. The constables saluted as they scooted out, amused grins pasted on delighted faces.

"We've arrested Margaret."

"Yeah, I know. I was there," Felton said. "What for?"

"For the murder of Elsie," he answered, although the man already knew.

"Why am I here?"

"I have questions. Do you want a lawyer, Felton?" Gibson asked.

"Why? I didn't do anything." He coughed.

Gibson pushed the recorder on.

"Do you know why Margaret murdered Elsie?"

"No. Did she?" Felton hesitated before continuing. "It'll be Elsie's fault for getting killed. She's nothing but a gossipmonger."

Gibson urged his lips together, bearing the fury he felt at the despicable man. Felton accepted the detective's gag for approval.

"She spreads rumours like I smear peanut butter." His snicker changed into a fit of whooping. He tugged out his grubby handkerchief and added to its ghastly stench. Gibson remained restrained, letting the aged fellow babble on.

"Ten years ago, she claimed I was a paedophile. Suggested I had something to do with…" He clamped his trap shut and launched a sneaky look toward the detective.

"With what Felton?"

"Nothing, Gibson." He dragged out the word into a drawl and coughed.

"So, what happened lately that changed things?"

"Gregory is what happened."

"What like father, like son?" Gibson recalled what Jackie had heard.

"Yeah, something like that."

"Tell me, Felton, where did the rape happen?" Not that it was relevant, but he was curious.

"At the beach." Felton's black eyes drilled into his steely grey eyes.

"What? At Lawsons Lane?" The answer surprised Gibson. He tried to connect the dots while Felton rambled on.

"Who does she think she is? Accusing me of whatever. Moreover, Gregory didn't even rape anyone. So the hell with that father and son bullshit." He stopped and wiggled in his chair, sliding down further into its tortuous hardness. His face had turned crimson. "It's all because the victim was a kid Elsie knew."

The inspector's cell trilled. "Gibson." He listened for a while, his mouth twitching with anticipation. "You're sure. Blue." He hung up.

"Where do you fit in, Felton?" Gibson asked, trying to keep his tone detached.

"I don't," he answered, struggling to bolt out of his seat, but choked instead. "What bullshit!" Felton gobbed into his bandana. The coughing ceased for a time. He mopped his mouth and cleared his throat. It sent him into a fit. He clutched at his chest.

Gibson got up. He hollered down the corridor. "Hey, Cooper. Get us some water." The old man continued to gag. "Stat."

"Here you go boss." Cooper came around the corner a second later.

Felton gulped down the cool liquid and collected himself. "I've had enough of this crap." He licked his tobacco-stained lips.

"A few more questions, if you don't mind," Gibson said. He stared at the drained glass. Well water. Felton's house next to the beach access. The tumultuous thoughts that had trundled through his mind and nagged suddenly came together—to just one outcome that made sense. "Should we search for Katie's body at your place?" The pit-bull snarled at him.

"What? No," Felton shouted.

"In the pump house?" Gibson bared his teeth.

Felton's unsavoury pallor waned further. He spat on the floor.

Gibson stuck his head out the door and yelled, "Cooper."

"What's going on?" Eckhart looked up at the screeching and bustled down the hallway from her vigilance.

"They found some blue shorts in the pumphouse," Gibson said as he stepped out into the corridor.

"So?" Eckhart said.

"A child's size. Dilapidated." He thought of the file and the description of blue shorts the young girl had worn. "It's a long shot but what if Katie didn't drown?"

"What? You're kidding. Margaret?"

"No. Felton. Everything seems to be linked to that beach."

"What does that mean?" she asked.

"I'm not sure. But a DNA test will tell us if the shorts are Katie's."

"Why would Felton keep them? Some kind of souvenir?"

"That's right. He has a history of sexual misconduct. Remember," Gibson replied.

Eckhart nodded.

"Yes, sir." The constable sprinted toward them and skidded to an abrupt standstill in front of Gibson.

"Call your guys at the house. Tell them to search further in the pump house."

Cooper inclined his head in query.

"With shovels," Gibson said.

"Sir."

"They'll be looking for bones. Old bones. Of an adolescent."

"Whoa. Right away," Cooper replied. He flipped a salute and was about to charge off when a commotion snared his attention. Felton had scraped his chair along the floor and lunged at Gibson, slamming him into the metal doorframe.

"Let me out of here. You, asshole," he shouted.

"Get this man locked up first," Gibson said. He seized the old man gruffly by the wrist and shoved him over to the DC. As Cooper dragged him down the corridor to the cells at the rear of the station, Felton howled, wailed and cursed.

"You can't do this to me. She stumbled and struck her head. It wasn't my fault..." Felton bit down on his lip.

Gibson ran after him.

"What did you say?"

"Nothing. I did nothing," he whined. His face glistened in the muddy light. His lips were chapped and raw, a dribble of blood stuck on his sharp chin.

"You did nothing all right. Not a thing to save Katie. You make…"

Cooper thrust Felton into a four-walled white box. The gate clanged shut, and with a flourish of the key the detainee was secured. He took a backward glance and snorted. Felton remained huddled on the concrete, coughing and gasping for breath.

"I'm going to die in here," he whimpered. His body shivered in the midst of the heatwave.

"Die, you bastard," Cooper mumbled behind his hand. He kicked at the floor as he left and headed to the house at the end of Lawsons Lane.

Gibson shook himself off and proceeded to the front desk.

"Get a doctor in there for Felton. We have to do it right. The man needs some medical attention," he said.

"You bet," the dispatcher replied and picked up the phone.

* * *

Eckhart leaned on the counter, already starting on the mounds of reports that needed to be done. She looked up when Gibson approached.

"Margaret won't say a word," she said.

"Felton made up for it." His cell buzzed. "Okay. Yes." He hung up.

"Keep me in suspense," Eckhart said.

"They found bones."

"That quick?"

"Felton didn't stash them deep. The forensic anthropologist is on her way. We'll find out in a few hours."

"Oh, my god." She held her palm to her mouth. "Is it Katie?"

"Not certain if the bones are even human at this point," he replied. "My flight is still hours away. Should we go for a beer?"

"Sure." She hitched. "Gibson."

He looked at Eckhart.

"I'll drive you to the airport. No problem."

"Okay. Thanks. That would be really nice."

They bumped fists. The walk to the pub was stifling, but they didn't notice. They relaxed in silence, waiting for the call. After an hour, his cell chirped.

"Gibson." He nodded several times before hanging up, a stern expression on his face.

"They discovered a gingham blouse in the potting shed. It was rumpled and bloodstained."

"Margaret's blouse?"

"Yeah," Gibson answered.

"And Elsie's blood?"

"Presumably."

Eckhart clapped her hands. They had a bite to eat before the next call came.

"Gibson." He listened attentively before hanging up.

"The bones are human from a young girl about ten."

"Oh, shit," Eckhart exclaimed.

"They're collecting the bones now. Frenchy is there too. They'll take them to the lab. But it'll take some time before they can identify them as Katie's," Gibson said.

"I know." Eckhart closed her eyes and looked in her heart. "If they are, I'll have to notify the Underwoods. Won't I?"

"Yes, no getting around that," he answered. Gibson didn't envy her that task. "Regardless. You have two murderers. Two cases."

Eckhart buried her face with her hands.

"You'll be okay," he reached over and touched her arm. "You have excellent people working for you."

"I do."

They finished up and drifted back to the station. Brown-shoes was seated on the bench that Gibson had deserted hours before. His briefcase lay flopped at his feet on the dirty, cracked linoleum. He looked up at the swish of the door.

"Inspector."

"Yes." Gibson towered over the shrivelling figure.

"May I have a word with you?" Brown-shoes asked as he grappled to rise.

"You are?" Although Gibson knew who the lawyer was.

"Philip Smith. Margaret wishes to make a statement."

"Okay." Gibson glanced at Eckhart. He cloaked his mouth to disguise the grin.

They followed Philip as he shuffled down the corridor to an interview room where his client had been cooling her heels. Margaret's Brillo hair was greyer and flatter now. She fidgeted in her chair, her ample thighs sagging over the narrow plastic seat and her bare ankles swollen into knobs of fat. Philip sat next to her, his eyebrows looked like a fuzzy caterpillar stuck on his forehead. Eckhart took a seat by the door and stayed quiet. Gibson sat down and slapped the recorder on.

"Did you kill Elsie?"

Margaret clawed at the mole on her beak and worked her mouth, the trace of spittle at the corners growing larger.

"Go ahead, Margaret," Philip said and brushed her scaly hand.

"It was an accident," she replied. Her pudgy fingers gripped the rim of the table.

Gibson waited, his smoky eyes turning to steel.

"It was the final straw." Margaret sat up straight, indignant at being quizzed about her actions. "She attacked us. Well, Felton for years." She stopped and found her voice again. "First it was about Katie. Then Gregory was arrested. Elsie wouldn't shut up."

Her eyes burned holes into the wood surface of the table.

Philip altered his position. His neck wobbled.

"I was in the kitchen getting a beer for Felton at the fireworks. I saw Elsie walking to the beach access so I thought I would finally confront her. It needed doing. I took our pathway down to the beach. I asked her to stop gossiping about us. To leave us alone. Just that morning she had been going on about my family. She wouldn't listen to me. She spun away and laughed. I seized her arm. I was only going to talk to her," Margaret rambled endlessly. "She lashed out at me. She slipped."

Gibson stared.

"It was an accident. Will you help me?" Margaret pleaded. Her face had gone beet red with the exertion. Her chin jiggled independently from the poison coming from her mouth.

"It wasn't an accident. I can't help you," Gibson replied and turned off the recorder.

A sour stench of old age and fear pervaded Eckhart's nostrils. The odour emanated from Margaret and penetrated the tiny space. Gibson stood up and called for an officer. Two uniforms came at once, rushing into the stale room.

"Get her out of here."

The detectives escaped the room.

"What? Did she expect we were going to let her have a pass?" Eckhart asked. "Duh."

"I have no idea about that but I do about something else," Gibson said.

"Oh."

"I think the ring is Gregory's."

"What? That's no good. Is it?" Her eyebrows furrowed in confusion.

"What I mean to say is, I believe Gregory left his ring at home when he went to jail."

"Okay," Eckhart said, not quite following his thoughts.

"The ring wasn't dirty or scarred in any way. Remember how shiny it was when Frenchy showed it to us at the lab."

"So?"

"So I don't think it was lost some other time, and I don't think Gregory lost it either," Gibson said.

"Where are you going with this?"

"I think Margaret had the ring cleaned and polished, and she had it with her when she killed Elsie. Probably in a pocket."

"And she planned to give it to her son at the party. Sort of a coming home present," Eckhart finished his sentence.

"Exactly. Why don't you find out where Margaret had the ring cleaned? If I were you, I would go to the jewelry store at Grantham Plaza. That's the closet one."

"I think you could be right," Eckhart replied. "I know the place."

"Good."

"We should leave soon. Get you to the airport," Eckhart said, as she glanced at her watch.

"I'm ready."

Eckhart cruised down the Queen Elizabeth Highway with the sun behind them, just about to plunge below the horizon. Soft music played on the radio. Eckhart hummed along with the songs, tapping her fingernails on the steering wheel. Gibson pressed into the backrest. He closed his eyes and sailed off. The Expedition hopped the curb.

"I guess we're there." He chuckled.

Eckhart slanted her head and threw him a sweet smile, a hint of affection.

Gibson acknowledged with a nod.

"Stay in touch."

"You bet."

He looked backward after she drew away, then scurried out of the heat into the terminal. It was a short wait before the plane took off for Victoria. He stared out the tiny window at the city lights below. In the western sky, sunlight lingered where Katherine waited. A new life would shortly be part of his family. Gibson fell asleep to the purr of the engines.

If you enjoyed this book, please let others know by leaving a quick review on Amazon. Also, if you spot anything untoward in the paperback, get in touch. We strive for the best quality and appreciate reader feedback.

editor@thebookfolks.com

Sign up to our mailing list to find out about other great books, new releases and special offers!

www.thebookfolks.com

More books in this series

MURDER ON VANCOUVER ISLAND
(Book 1)

Inspector Gibson cuts short a jaunt in his beloved kayak to attend a murder inquiry. The investigation soon meets a brick wall, but he suspects the victim's co-workers are involved. He must act quickly before the case, like the weather, goes cold.

MURDER ON THE SAANICH PENINSULA
(Book 3)

When a woman is murdered, Inspector William Gibson immediately suspects her husband is responsible. His junior partner is not so sure. But when the truth emerges it has a knock-on effect that will change the detective's life for ever. And not in a good way.

Printed in Great Britain
by Amazon